NANTUCKET WEDDINGS

PAMELA M. KELLEY

PIPING PLOVER PRESS

This story is dedicated in memory of my grandfather, Ken Ford, who was also a writer and a poet and the inspiration for the character Ken in this story.

INTRODUCTION

Mia Maxwell used to have her dream job. She is a sought after wedding planner on Nantucket, with no shortage of business. But she is struggling a bit to get back to loving her job. It has been bittersweet to plan other people's weddings--ever since her own fiance died two weeks before their wedding.

That was a year ago and she was just starting to feel better, when she came back from a vacation to find her house burned down. So she will be staying with Lisa at the Beach Plum Cove Inn for a while, until her house is renovated.

Mia's also worried about her younger sister and best friend Izzy--she has a serious boyfriend who has grown more controlling over the past year.

As it turns out, there are several members of the Hodges family that may be in need of Mia's services-- she'll be planning not one but two weddings. There are a few road bumps along the way however.

Lisa has another long-term guest that she eagerly introduces to Mia. She finds this temporary neighbor equally intriguing and frustrating and she makes it clear that she's not even close to ready to date. She's not sure if she ever will be.

CHAPTER 1

Spring was Lisa Hodges' favorite season on Nantucket. It was warm enough to take long walks on the beach, and to smell the salty air and to pick some gorgeous tulips. She put them in a pretty vase when she went into her kitchen and set them in the dining room so her guests would be able to enjoy them.

It was Saturday morning and as usual, Lisa was up early. She'd already baked a ham and asparagus quiche and walked along the beach for about a half hour, while the quiche was in the oven. Only half of the rooms were rented as it was still early in the season. When the quiche was ready, she brought it into the dining room and set it on a heated plate. Cut fruit, bagels and cream cheese followed.

The girls, her twin thirty-something daughters, Kristen and Kate, arrived a few minutes apart, as Lisa was bringing a hot thermos of coffee and a basket of creamers into the dining room. Her youngest, Abby, was the last to arrive, with Lisa's granddaughter, Natalie, in a stroller. Every Saturday, whenever possible, the girls came for breakfast with Lisa.

Lisa's live-in fiancé, Rhett, joined them as well, but as usual, he just had coffee to start, while everyone else loaded their plates with quiche and a bit of everything else.

As they ate, talk turned to local gossip, as it always did.

"How is your friend, Mia, doing?" Lisa asked Kate. She'd read about the condo fire at the pier. It was a blessing that Mia had been out of town, and that no one was hurt.

"She's hanging in there. This past year has been rough, and now the fire. I don't think she's loving living with her sister, though. She said she's been looking around to find a short-term rental for a month or two."

Lisa thought about that for a minute. She liked Mia. She was quiet and hard-working. And she was doing a wonderful job planning Kate's upcoming wedding.

"Have her give me a call. I should be able to give her a room if she's interested."

Kate looked surprised and pleased. "Really? That would be great." She hesitated a moment before adding, "she has a dog, though. Penny is a Pomeranian. She's adorable and tiny, but I'm not sure what your thoughts are on that?"

Lisa considered it, then smiled. "I think that would be okay. As long as she behaves herself. Those are usually good dogs."

MIA MAXWELL HAD LOST COUNT OF HOW MANY PEOPLE had assured her that the first year was the hardest. And that it would get easier after that.

She knew they meant well. But she was still waiting. They were right that the first year was hard, but she'd sort of expected the fog to lift on the one-year mark. Instead, her feelings were still murky, cloudy, foggy as ever.

The vacation was supposed to help. And it did, briefly. She went to Charleston, one of her favorite places in the world, to visit one of her favorite people, her college roommate, Alicia. The weather was wonderful, the food amazing—she ate shrimp and grits everywhere.

And she had felt well-rested as she glanced out the airport window waiting to board the small Cape Air plane—the nine-seater that shuttled passengers from Boston to Nantucket. Spring in Nantucket was always a season of hope—tulips and daffodils blooming, pink blossoms on cherry trees and retail shops opening for the summer season.

She'd been looking forward to relaxing in her condo —her oasis of calm. The two-bedroom townhouse on the pier was an easy walk everywhere downtown. She'd redecorated over the past year, as a way to focus on something other than the premature death of Mark Anderson, her fiancé. Her sister, Izzy, was the creative one in the family and helped her choose the colors. They went with soft creams, and misty sea tones of pale green and blue.

Shortly before she boarded the flight, Izzy had called,

hysterical, to tell her about the fire. They still weren't sure how it had started. Electrical was the best guess, but Mia's end unit and the one next to it suffered the most damage. So, instead of hunkering down at home, on her soft ivory-colored sofa, under a cuddly fleece throw, she and her beloved dog, Penny, moved into Izzy's guest bedroom.

And that wasn't working out so well. Mia was grateful that Izzy had insisted she stay with her and her boyfriend of almost a year, Rick Savage. But after three days, Mia knew for the sake of her sanity and her relationship with her sister that she had to find her own place. The renovation could last several months, and her insurance would cover alternate housing. Izzy's place was just too small. Well, that wasn't entirely true. If it was just Izzy, it would have been fine. Mia just couldn't handle Rick, and the way he treated Izzy. It was eye-opening and disturbing. She'd seen a side of him that he'd kept hidden. And Mia didn't want to be around it.

So, she started looking for another option and wasn't having any luck until her friend Kate called. She'd mentioned to Kate that she was looking for something and was surprised when Kate called to suggest her mother's inn. Lisa Hodges had converted her waterfront home into an inn, since she no longer needed five extra bedrooms and she did need a source of income. Mia tried not to get too excited, as she wasn't sure if she'd be able to afford a room there.

But when Mia called, the rate that Lisa quoted was reasonable and she explained that for monthly rentals she was able to go a little below the market rate. It fit into what Mia's insurance would cover, and she assured Lisa that her dog would behave. Penny was almost nine years old, and she was a good girl. Mia took a drive by Lisa's house and knew that Penny would love walking on that beach. And Mia knew the walking would do her good, too.

Now, she just had to figure out the best way to explain to her sister why she didn't want to stay there any longer and why she thought her sister should leave, too. But she knew that part of the conversation was for another day.

CHAPTER 2

Izzy was cooking something that smelled delicious when Mia walked through the door. It had been a long day with two particularly fussy brides, and she was eager to kick her shoes off and relax. She looked around the room and didn't see Rick, so that was a relief. But then she heard a cough and realized he was just down the hall in their office. Izzy looked up when she saw her sister and smiled.

"Hope you're hungry. I made a ton of food."

"I'm starving. What is that? It smells amazing."

"Just something I threw together—pasta with lots of garlic, white wine, sliced chicken and grilled artichokes out of a can from Trader Joe's. That's the secret ingredient."

Mia felt her stomach rumble. "Sounds great. Do you feel like a glass of wine? I'm going to have one." Izzy nodded, and Mia opened a bottle and poured a glass for each of them. "Do you think Rick will want one?"

"What will Rick want?" Mia almost jumped at the deep voice that was suddenly behind her. She hadn't heard him walk over.

"Cabernet."

"Sure, I'll take a glass. Why not?"

She handed him a glass of wine, and he took it and settled at the kitchen table, waiting for dinner to be served.

"Can I do anything to help?" Mia offered.

"No, go sit and relax. I'm just going to plate this up." Izzy filled two large bowls with pasta for Mia and Rick and set them on the table, then returned with one for herself and a big loaf of bread on a cutting board. Mia jumped up and grabbed the butter, then settled back down again. The food was delicious and as they ate, Izzy chattered away telling them about her day. She owned a small shop on Main Street, and Mia was so proud of how well she'd done. Izzy had always had a flair for fashion, and the ability to pull simple pieces together in a way that looked stylish and unique.

Her shop was an eclectic mix of high-end one-of-a-kind pieces and less expensive pretty tops and dresses, as well as some Nantucket basics like well-made sweatshirts with Nantucket stamped across the front. Izzy often lamented that there were plenty of days where the sweatshirts were her top sellers as her shop was near the pier and people often wandered in after arriving on the ferries.

"I think I had as many dogs in the shop today as I did customers. I think just about everyone that comes to the island these days brings their dog," Izzy said.

"I can't believe you let them in the shop. Seems like you're asking for trouble," Rick said as he reached for a slice of bread.

But Izzy just laughed. "The dogs are never a problem. They're generally better behaved than their owners."

They all had second helpings of the pasta and as they were almost done eating, Mia took a deep breath and broke the news.

"So, I'll be out of your hair soon. Tomorrow, actually. Kate Hodges put me in touch with her mother, Lisa, who runs the Beach Plum Cove Inn and she has a room for me, at a rate that works for my insurance."

Izzy immediately looked dismayed and set her fork down. "You don't have to do that. I love having you here."

"It looks like the renovation work could take longer than we initially thought. It could go for several months. I can't impose on you guys that long. And insurance covers it."

"I hate to see you stay in an inn, when you could be here with us," Izzy said.

"Maybe Mia wants her space," Rick said. "I can't say that I blame her. This place is kind of small for three people." Izzy shot a warning look at Rick, but he didn't seem to notice.

"You'll have to come visit. Lisa said they have breakfast every morning. It's right on the water. We can go for a walk on the beach."

"Well, if you're sure that's what you want to do?"

"I think it's the best thing." Mia couldn't wait to move

out. She would miss her sister, but Rick was right. The place felt crowded with the three of them.

Mia helped Izzy clear the table, while Rick went through a stack of mail on the counter. He'd been in a relatively good mood during dinner. But Mia felt a shift in the air as he opened a bill and stared at it a bit too long.

"Izzy, I thought you said you paid the electric?" There was an edge to his voice that Mia recognized, and she glanced at her sister.

Izzy turned off the water and smiled. "I thought I did."

"This says otherwise. It's past due and scheduled for shutoff on Tuesday."

Izzy bit her lower lip. "I'm sorry. I could have sworn I paid that. I meant to." Mia didn't doubt that Izzy meant to, but she knew her sister was prone to forget things like that. She'd never been very good about paying bills on time, even when she had the money for them.

Rick pulled a checkbook from a drawer and angrily ripped off a check. He filled it out and stuffed it in his wallet.

"It's taken care of now. I'll drop it off tomorrow on my way to work."

"Thank you, Rick." Izzy's voice was soft, and Mia knew she was embarrassed.

He stared at her for a long, uncomfortable moment before finally having the last word. "It's really pathetic, you know. It's a good thing our power didn't get shut off."

Izzy didn't say anything, while Mia glared at Rick. He topped off his glass with more wine, then smiled as if he hadn't just been a complete jerk. "I'm going to watch the game in the other room."

As soon as he was out of earshot, Mia refilled both her and Izzy's glasses and brought them into the living room. They settled on the sofa and Penny jumped up between them, flopped down and looked at Mia expectantly. Mia reached over and petted her while Izzy clicked on the TV.

"I don't like the way he talks to you," Mia said softly. She didn't want to get into a big discussion with her sister, as she knew Rick could walk back into the room at any moment. But she had to say something.

Izzy sighed. "He has his moments, but he's been under a lot of stress lately. I think things are tough at work right now." Rick had recently started a new job, as an electrician with a local company. He'd been laid off from his prior employer, and Mia couldn't help but wonder if he was difficult to work with.

"Well, if you ever want a break, you're welcome to stay with me. Anytime."

Izzy smiled. "Thanks. It might be fun to have a girls' night sometime."

"Let's plan on it."

CHAPTER 3

"Nantucket Weddings. This is Mia." Her phone rang just as Mia reached The Beach Plum Cove Inn the next morning.

"Mia, it's Bethany Billings. I ran into your mother at the Met Gala last week and she said I had to call you. I just got engaged and we want to get married on Nantucket. Our family has a summer cottage there."

Mia smiled. She'd gone to the Spence School, an exclusive private school on the Upper East Side in New York City with Bethany. The Billings' family 'cottage' was a sprawling seaside mansion. Mia had known Bethany, but they hadn't been close friends and it had been years since she'd talked to her.

"That's wonderful. Congratulations. I'd be happy to help. Have you set a date?"

"Three months from now. August fifteenth. I know that's soon, but we really don't want to wait. We've been dating forever."

"Well, a late summer wedding on Nantucket will be lovely. We can make it happen."

"Thank goodness." Bethany sounded relieved. "I did try for something in the city at first, but then we decided on Nantucket." Mia knew it would be impossible to put on the kind of wedding Bethany's family would want in the city on such short notice.

"Are you free around eleven tomorrow morning? I can stop by and we can go over everything."

"Perfect." Mia jotted down her address, parked and told Penny she'd be right back. She wanted to get the key to her room before bringing Penny and her bags inside.

Lisa answered the door a moment after Mia knocked.

"Hi, Mia." Lisa opened the door wide and Mia followed her in.

She'd met Lisa for the first time a few months back when she and Kate met to discuss Kate's wedding. Mia had been struck then by the resemblance to her friend, Kate. Lisa had the same color hair, big eyes and friendly smile. Lisa's hair fell in a long bob just to her shoulders and was tucked behind her ears for an overall preppy look that was common on Nantucket.

"I'm so sorry about the fire. Do they know what caused it?" Lisa asked once they reached the kitchen.

"They are still investigating, but it sounds like it may have been an accident. Something to do with work being done. I'm not really sure."

"Well, at least no one was hurt. I think I read that the unit next to yours was empty at the time, too?"

Mia nodded. "It was actually just sold, but the new owners hadn't moved in yet."

"Oh, no! How awful for them."

Mia hadn't thought much about it as she'd been so wrapped up in her own problems, but Lisa was right. A fire would be a terrible thing to have happen to a home you hadn't even moved into yet. She was just grateful that Penny hadn't been there at the time. She'd debated whether to have her sister stop by to feed Penny while she was gone and was glad that Izzy had insisted on bringing Penny to stay with her. She knew Penny would be less lonely and as it turned out she was much safer, too. Mia handed Lisa a check for the first month's rent and she tucked it into a kitchen drawer.

"Thank you. Let's head upstairs and I'll show you to your room. Did you bring your dog?"

"Penny's in the car. I'll run and get her so you can meet her, too."

Mia went and got Penny and brought her inside a few minutes later. Lisa immediately bent down to pet her.

"She's adorable!" Penny lifted her head and twitched her tail, approving immediately of Lisa. Penny liked just about everyone.

They followed Lisa upstairs and she unlocked room number four, which faced the ocean. Mia let out a happy sigh when Lisa swung the door open. The room was perfect. It was spacious and pretty with pale yellow bedding, navy and white curtains and a big bathroom with white bead board. The overall feel was crisp and clean and beachy. A corner of the room was set up like a mini-kitchen, with a refrigerator and microwave and a small table and chair by the window. Lisa followed her gaze.

"I just had the Wifi upgraded, and it's much faster now. There's maid service in the morning and breakfast downstairs from eight to ten. Here's your key. Don't hesitate to let me know if you need anything."

"Thank you. I'll probably see you at breakfast tomorrow."

Lisa smiled. "I look forward to it. I hope you'll be very comfortable here."

After Lisa left, Mia brought her bags in from the car and spent the next hour settling in, unpacking and putting her clothes in the chest of drawers and closet. Penny sat on the bed and watched. When Mia finished, she decided to go for a walk on the beach.

"Want to go outside?" Penny's tail immediately twitched, and she jumped off the bed and ran to the door. Mia got her leash, hooked her up and off they went. It was a lovely day. The sun was shining, and it was warm enough that she only needed a light jacket. The beach was mostly empty except for a few other walkers and dogs. Mia strolled the length of the beach, stopping now and then so Penny could sniff around, or walk in circles before doing her business, which Mia immediately scooped up with one of the plastic bags that she always kept in her coat pocket.

A half hour later, they returned to the house. Mia took a deep breath before stepping inside. The air was cool and had a fresh, clean smell. It was instantly calming, and she was glad that she'd made the decision to move out of Izzy's place. She hadn't slept well the night before, and when she climbed the stairs, unlocked her door and stepped inside, a wave of exhaustion swept over her. The bed looked comfortable, and it seemed like a really good idea to lay down for just a minute.

She took her shoes off, then sprawled on the bed and pulled the soft comforter over her. Penny jumped up and settled on the pillow next to her. Mia reached over and petted her for a moment, then closed her eyes and let herself sink into a deep sleep.

She woke with a start and was surprised to see when she checked the time that almost two hours had passed. After a moment of panic, she relaxed and pulled her covers tighter around her. Her schedule was clear for the rest of the day. There was no one she needed to call or go see. Nothing until the next day at eleven.

There was plenty that she could do—fiddle with ads, follow up with people that had requested information a while back to see if they were close to a decision. But the thought of doing anything like that just made her more exhausted. Sometimes she fought these feelings, and other times she gave in.

Slowly, she swung her legs out from under the covers, stood and walked over to the window and stared out at the ocean, at the waves crashing against the shore. She cracked the window open a few inches and could hear the soothing sounds as the tide came in and rushed out again. Her eyes fell on the Keurig coffee maker and a small bowl with a few coffee pods and tea bags. Maybe a hot cup of tea would help her to come back to life a bit.

While the machine whirred and groaned as it heated up the hot water, Mia felt a wave of sadness rush over her. Her eyes welled up as she thought for the millionth time of her last day with Mark. It had been a Saturday afternoon, and she'd been sipping coffee and staring out the window of her condo, watching the boat traffic along the pier. Mark had walked up behind her, wrapped his arms around her waist and kissed the side of her neck. She loved when he did that and she leaned into him, feeling safe and happy in his arms.

He'd died less than an hour later. While she'd been visiting with her sister, he'd taken his new motorcycle for a ride. They said he'd been killed instantly by a food delivery truck heading for Stop and Shop. Mark had taken a corner maybe a little too fast, hit a patch of sand and slid right into the truck head on. The truck driver was devastated. It happened so fast that he didn't have time to get out of the way. It had been such a perfect day, and then just like that, it was over.

It still often didn't seem real. So often, Mia reached for the phone to call Mark when something good or funny happened, before realizing that she couldn't call him ever again. And just like that her good mood would vanish, like a candle that had been snuffed out. It happened far less often now, but still from time to time, her mind seemed to forget that a year had passed, and the hurt would be fresh and raw again.

But, for the most part, it was getting somewhat easier.

Mia forced herself to focus on happy thoughts as she sipped her tea, and her mood lifted. When she finished, she took a hot shower, dressed in her favorite old jeans and faded baby blue sweatshirt, blew her long blond hair dry and felt almost like a new person.

She took Penny with her as she ran some errands, going to the post office and supermarket to pick up some groceries, simple things like cold cuts, and soups she could heat up easily in the microwave. She worked a little for the rest of the afternoon, planning the rest of her week, and by dinner time, she decided to treat herself with takeout from Millie's, which had the best scallop and bacon tacos.

She took Penny out for another walk along the beach after she ate and then settled in for the night with a good book and a little TV. After drifting off to sleep around eleven, she woke soon after to the sound of a woman's scream and a loud crash in the hallway. She jumped out of bed and opened the door, concerned that someone might be hurt, and stopped short when she saw a woman about her age, struggling to her feet and laughing somewhat hysterically while a tall man with almost black hair fumbled with his key in the door next to hers. They both looked her way when her door opened and the woman laughed again, followed by a loud hiccup. The man looked apologetic.

"I'm so sorry. We'll keep it down, I promise."

Mia just nodded and watched as he swung his door open and helped the woman who seemed somewhat unsteady on her feet, get up and inside. The man looked vaguely familiar, but she couldn't place him. She closed her door and climbed back in bed. There was no more noise from the room next door, and Mia soon relaxed and fell back asleep.

MIA WOKE EARLY THE NEXT MORNING, A LITTLE BEFORE seven, and felt rested and fully relaxed for the first time since she'd come back from her vacation. She'd left the window open a crack and fell asleep to the sound of the ocean. Penny stirred when Mia woke and once she changed, she took her out for a walk along the beach. They walked for almost an hour, the full length of the beach down to a pretty lighthouse and back. And by the time they reached the house, Mia was starving.

She set out food for Penny and then made her way downstairs to the dining room. It was just a few minutes past eight and she hoped it wasn't too early. But Lisa was already in the room, pouring herself a cup of coffee. She looked up and smiled when she saw Mia.

"Good morning. Help yourself to coffee and juice. We have a bacon and cheese quiche today, some fresh fruit, muffins and bagels."

Mia poured a mug of coffee, added a slice of quiche and some cantaloupe slices to a plate and sat down across from Lisa. A moment later, an older man joined them, but he just had a cup of black coffee. Lisa introduced them.

"Mia, this is my fiancé, Rhett."

Rhett nodded and sipped his coffee silently while Lisa and Mia chatted. An older couple came in a few minutes later and joined them, too. They introduced themselves as Al and Betty Smith and they were excited to head out for a day of sightseeing.

"It's our first time on Nantucket," Betty said. "We're thinking of seeing the Whaling Museum first and then shop for a bit before lunch. Al wants to do a walking ghost tour tonight. I wasn't sure about that. What do you think?"

"I haven't done the ghost tour, but people seem to enjoy it. The Whaling Museum is wonderful," Lisa said.

Mia nodded. "I agree. And you can spend a few hours there. I did the walking ghost tour a few years ago, and I really liked it. There's a lot of history and it's a little spooky. Supposedly, Nantucket is very haunted."

"See, I told you it would be fun," Al said.

Betty laughed. "All right, ghost tour it is."

They left a few minutes later, taking their muffins with them. Mia lingered over a second cup of coffee and helped herself to another sliver of quiche after Lisa encouraged her.

"I'm hungrier than usual this morning. Penny and I went for a long walk on the beach. It's really beautiful here."

Lisa smiled. "Thank you. I usually get a good walk in most mornings. Helps me feel less guilty about having that second slice."

They chatted a bit more and when they finished eating, Lisa glanced toward the door. "I thought your neighbor would have been down by now. I wanted to introduce him to you. He seems like a nice young man, and about your age."

Mia doubted her neighbor and his friend were going to be up any time soon.

"I heard him come home late last night. I wouldn't count on him making it down for breakfast."

"Oh, that's too bad. Well, I believe he's going to be here for a while, too. Funny thing, he checked in a week ago, but told me yesterday that he just closed on the condo next to yours, right before the fire. So, he's having renovations done too and has extended his stay. What a small world it is."

"Really? That's interesting. What is his name? I wonder if I know him."

"Ben. Ben Billings. His family owns a place here, but he said the whole family is in town and his sister is planning a wedding and it's too crazy for him there."

Mia smiled. So, that's where she knew him from. It had been years since she'd seen Ben Billings. He'd been two years ahead of her and had gone to Buckley, the nearby private boy's school. She didn't know him well, but she knew of him. Everyone knew Ben Billings. He'd been taller, better looking, and richer than just about everyone. And even in high school, he'd had a reputation for dating pretty much anyone he wanted to. He was always in the society pages, going to all the important events, always with a different beautiful girl. So, she was surprised to hear that Ben was the buyer of the condo next to hers. She couldn't imagine that he'd want to be on Nantucket for more than a few weeks.

Which was actually a good thing. She had an end unit, and if Ben wasn't going to be there much, it would be nice and quiet. Just the way she liked it. And given the way he'd come home last night, it looked like Ben was the same as ever.

"I'm actually on my way to meet with his sister later this morning. She wants me to help with her wedding."

Lisa's eyes lit up. "How fun. I look forward to hearing more about it. I bet it will be a fancy one."

Mia laughed. "Yes, I think it probably will be."

CHAPTER 4

At a quarter to eleven, Mia drove onto the long, winding driveway that led to the Billings' oceanfront summer home. As she came around the corner and saw the sprawling white house and expansive manicured lawn, she wondered if Bethany had considered having the wedding there. It would be a lovely setting, with breathtaking views of the ocean.

She parked next to a white Range Rover and made her way to the front door. Bethany swung the door open a moment after Mia rang the bell. She looked almost the same as Mia remembered, with shiny, straight blonde hair and expertly cut long layers that fell just past her shoulders. Her eyes were big and blue, and her lashes long and fake. But they were very good fakes. Her lipstick was a pretty shade of pink and when she smiled, her teeth were perfectly white. She was wearing a Lilly Pulitzer sundress in bright shades of peach and pink. And she was tan, very tan. Mia felt pale in comparison.

"Mia! It's so great to see you!" Bethany pulled her in for an enthusiastic hug as if they were long-lost friends.

"You, too."

"Come in! My mother is going to join us in a bit. I hope you're hungry. We thought you could stay for lunch?"

"Sure. Thank you." Mia didn't have anything pressing the rest of the day.

Bethany led her into a screened-in sunroom that had stunning ocean views. A big round table was set with a pot of coffee, cream and sugar and a plate of what looked like homemade chocolate chip cookies. A stack of bridal magazines sat next to the cookies. Once they were both seated, Bethany poured coffee for both of them and encouraged Mia to try the cookies.

"Our housekeeper, Dorothy, made them this morning and they are insanely good. I had one, which was more than I should have. But have as many as you want."

Mia nibbled one cookie and then another as Bethany chatted non-stop about what she envisioned for her wedding. Mia took notes, stopping now and then to clarify or to ask a question. Bethany mentioned that she wanted her reception at the Whitley Hotel, which was exquisite, but no more so than her own location.

"Have you considered having it here? You have plenty of room on the lawn and the views are spectacular. We could get tents and have it catered. It would be really lovely."

But Bethany made a face at the idea. "I did consider that, but no. The Whitley is perfect. With their rolling lawns, croquet and exceptional service and food, it's very Gatsby-esque. It will be just perfect."

Mia tried not to smile. Bethany's sprawling mansion was just as Gatsby-esque, but if she wanted the Whitley, Mia would happily make it happen.

Bethany glanced out the window. "I did think it might be nice to have a brunch here the next day, though. Maybe you could help with that and suggest a caterer?"

"Of course. There are a few that I work with often."

Bethany's mother, Lillian, joined them as Mia described the different caterers and their specialties. The resemblance between the two women was strong. Lillian had the same blonde hair, but hers was up in an elegant French twist. She wore a double strand of pearls around her neck, diamonds in her ears, and she was dressed head-to-toe in the palest yellow linen pants and a matching button-down shirt.

"I'm so glad you were available to help Bethany." Lillian smiled and her eyes were sympathetic as she added, "I'm so sorry about your fiancé. It's been almost a year now, I think your mother said?"

Mia nodded and felt a sharp pang of sadness at the mention of Mark.

"Thank you. Yes, it's been just over a year."

"I'm so sorry, Mia. I should have mentioned it earlier." Bethany looked distressed.

"Please, don't give it another thought. It's been hard, but it's getting easier as everyone told me it would." She hadn't expected Bethany to mention it as she hadn't seen her in forever, and she knew, like most brides, that

Bethany would be totally absorbed with her wedding and what she wanted.

Lillian nodded and changed the subject. "Your mother was telling me that you're a year-rounder on Nantucket now. It's lovely, but I can't imagine being here in the winter. It must be so quiet. Do you think you'll ever move back to the city?" Mia knew she meant Manhattan's Upper East Side, and Mia had no desire to live there again. So many assumed that Nantucket was deserted, desolate and deadly boring in the winter, but to Mia it was anything but.

She loved the hustle and bustle of summer, but always looked forward to the fall when the crowds thinned, but the weather was still gorgeous. And then winter was snug and peaceful. She enjoyed the calm of the off-season, followed by the hope that spring brought along with the cheery yellow daffodils that covered the island.

"I don't have any plans to move back there. I'm really happy here." She looked up as the door to the sunroom opened and three giggling teenage girls tumbled into the room.

"I'm not sure if you've met my younger sister, Lila? She just turned nineteen," Bethany said. Mia vaguely remembered that Lillian had divorced and remarried when Bethany was in high school.

"It's nice to meet you."

"Are you girls joining us for lunch?" Lillian asked.

But Lila shook her head. "We want to go into town and get pizza. Where are the keys to the Range Rover?"

"In the kitchen. But I'll need the car tonight, so be back around dinner time."

The girls spun around and went back the way they came in, chattering and laughing as they exited the room.

Lillian smiled. "I wish I had half their energy. Shall we go into the other room for lunch?"

Mia followed the two women into a pretty dining room with more gorgeous ocean views. Over a leisurely lunch of clam chowder and lobster salad sandwiches, served by their housekeeper, Lillian filled them in on all the city gossip. All the same people they knew that were engaged or having babies or having affairs. Even though Mia hadn't thought about any of these people in ages, it was still fun to hear what they were all up to. New York seemed like another world from the life she was living on Nantucket. She really didn't miss it.

"I bet your mother would love for you to move home?" Lillian said at one point.

And Mia laughed. "She does mention it often. I tell her that she should get out of the city more and come here. But she and my dad love the Hamptons. They have a place there."

"We used to go there. But I prefer to spend the summer here. My husband, Peter, flies in on the weekends. This year we have a full house. Both girls always have friends or boyfriends visiting and my son, Ben, decided to come this year, too, but he's not staying with us. He wanted his own place and bought a condo downtown, but then you heard about that fire?"

"Did someone say my name?" A booming voice came into the room along with the familiar face she'd seen the night before.

Lillian laughed. "Your ears must have been ringing. I was just telling Mia here about your condo—you remember Mia? She's helping with Bethany's wedding."

Ben stopped and stared at Mia for a moment and then broke into a grin. "Of course, I remember Mia. I think we're neighbors now, too—at the Beach Plum Cove Inn and eventually when our condos get fixed up."

Bethany wondered how he knew she was his neighbor at the condo, too. He must have noticed her confusion, and he explained, "I made it to breakfast late and Lisa filled me in."

"How interesting. You're going to be neighbors!" Bethany looked intrigued at the idea.

"Have you eaten? There's plenty of food. You could join us?" Lillian invited.

But Ben shook his head. "No, I'm not hungry. I just stopped in to pick up some insurance paperwork I had sent here that I need for the restoration. I'll catch up with you all later."

CHAPTER 5

Kate Hodges sighed as she stared at the blank computer screen. Her latest mystery just refused to write itself. She'd blasted through the first fifty pages, caught up in the excitement of her idea, which her trusted advisors—her fiancé Jack, her sisters, and Philippe, her good friend who was also a huge bestselling author, had all given the green light. But she was stuck and just didn't know what to do with these people next.

She stared past the computer and out the window at the gorgeous ocean views from where she sat in Jack's office, which had become her regular writing spot. The serene view usually inspired her. But not today—the water was choppy, the waves bigger than usual and topped with frothy whitecaps. It matched her mood, turbulent and unsettled.

She closed the laptop and stood and stretched. Maybe a walk around the block would help get some ideas flowing. She knew what the problem was. She was stressed out about her upcoming wedding and it was dampening her creativity. She pulled her hair into a ponytail, put her sneakers on and stepped outside.

Jack was at work, at the seafood market he helped his father run, and he wasn't due home until much later. He was going straight to his brother's place after work, and they were going to grab a beer and a bite to eat somewhere so that Kate could have the house for her girls' night gathering.

She was looking forward to seeing all of her favorite people, but she was also dreading the wedding-related questions that were bound to come up. Especially since she'd invited Mia, who was thankfully handling her wedding coordinating and was waiting patiently for answers to many of these questions. Her sisters, Kristen and Abby, her soon-to-be sister-in-law, Beth, who was marrying their younger brother, Chase, and their friend Angela, who was engaged to Philippe, were also coming.

Unlike her friend Mia, who lived and breathed weddings, and loved them so much she decided to make a career out of planning them, Kate had never been one of those girls that daydreamed about having a big wedding, who knew exactly what her dress would look like and what kind of cake she'd serve. Thinking about the many decisions she still needed to make was overwhelming, especially when it came to the guest list. She was dreading making the final call on who was a yes and who was a no.

If it was up to her and money was no object, she'd invite everyone they knew, but of course that wasn't realistic, especially on Nantucket where everything was more expensive, anyway. Jack had some uncles that needed sorting out. One was a definite yes and the other he hadn't seen in forever and had no interest in inviting, but technically he was Jack's godfather and his father was putting pressure on him to 'be nice' and just invite him. Kate had a good idea how that was going to turn out, but it was just one of many details that needed decisions. And she still had to pick out a dress. She'd tried on a bunch, but nothing had seemed right and they'd seen most of what was available on Nantucket, so a trip to the Cape, and probably to Boston, needed to happen soon.

Kate was excited to marry Jack, she just was dreading the wedding itself. She'd floated the idea of eloping or having a small, intimate family wedding and that had quickly been shot down by everyone. She knew her mother was looking forward to a bigger wedding so all their local friends and family could be there, and Jack had made it clear that his father expected the same. Especially as it didn't look as though Jack's brother would be getting married anytime soon, as he wasn't even dating anyone at the moment. Kate knew she'd probably have a wonderful time once the big day came. It was just getting to that point that was wearing on her.

It also didn't help that Sam Fisher had reached out to her only an hour ago via Facebook. That Sam Fisher. The one she'd been head-over-heels crazy about in high school. They'd dated for two years, freshman and sopho-more year, until his parents moved off-island, back to Wellesley, a suburb of Boston. They'd lost touch after a few months, and Kate hadn't thought about him in years. He'd sent her a friend request, followed by a message wanting to know if she'd like to meet for coffee, to catch up. Because he'd moved back to Nantucket.

His profile said he was married, with two children, and hers clearly showed she was engaged, so she didn't think anything of it. It would be fun to see Sam and to hear about his family and what had brought him back to Nantucket. She'd mention it to Jack, but she didn't think he'd have a problem with it. He wasn't the jealous type. She was glad, though, that Sam was married. If he'd been single and wanted to meet for coffee after all these years, she wasn't sure how she would have felt about that.

She started up the hill and hoped that after a fifteen- to twenty-minute walk, she'd have some idea of what needed to happen next in her story. And if that didn't work, she might just call it a day and start making her marinated tomatoes for her bruschetta topping. Everyone was bringing their favorite appetizers tonight, which was always fun, and Kate still needed to run to Bradford's Liquors to pick up a few more bottles of wine. A new Facebook message caught her attention as it flashed across her phone from Sam.

"Looking forward to catching up on Sunday. Meet you at eleven at The Bean?"

Kate smiled and immediately typed back. "Sounds good. See you then."

M<small>IA</small> <small>CHECKED</small> <small>HER</small> <small>PHONE</small> <small>WHEN</small> <small>SHE</small> <small>FINISHED</small> <small>WITH</small> Bethany and was back in her car. She quickly returned a few emails and listened to a message from Will Matthews, who was handling the fire damage removal and restoration for her condo. She smiled as she listened to the message.

"Hey, Mia. I'll be at the condo all afternoon if you want to stop by and take a look at some hard wood samples I found. Hope you're doing okay?" She texted him quickly. "I'm on my way now. Be there in fifteen minutes."

She was so glad that Will was doing the work. She trusted him and knew his work was excellent. He'd also been one of Mark's best friends, and they'd often spent time with Will and his fiancée, Caroline. Mia wasn't involved with that wedding. Caroline was doing everything herself. But she imagined she'd be getting an invite soon. She didn't remember the date Will had mentioned last, but thought it was probably coming up in the next few months.

When she pulled up to the condo and parked in one of her two designated parking spots, she saw that Will's truck was parked in the other one. She took a deep breath as she walked toward her front door. The first time she'd seen the condo after the fire had been such a shock. Even though most of the damage was on the second floor and the roof, there was still soot everywhere and the smoke stench had been almost unbearable. Everything stunk of smoke—it permeated her mattress, the carpet, all of her clothes. She'd had to throw it all out. Will had arranged to have everything else, her bed and other furniture, moved to a storage facility so it could air out and, if needed, he would then work to remove any lingering smoke smell.

Will had also suggested, instead of replacing the wall-to-wall carpeting, that she go with hardwood floors and she liked that idea. They were more durable, and she could choose different throw rugs in various colors to accent them. And in the remote chance there was ever a fire again, the wood could likely be salvaged, sanded down and refinished.

Her door was ajar, and she could hear Will hard at work. When she stepped inside, he was in the kitchen, scrubbing away at the very sooty walls. He turned at the sound of her footsteps, and pulled off the mask he wore to protect from the chemicals and soot flying around in the air. He ran a hand through his sandy blond hair, pushing it off his face. Will and Mark were such opposites in looks. Will was taller and thinner, with light skin, a dusting of freckles across his face and arms that were lean and muscled from working with his hands all day.

"Hey there. Come out on the deck and I'll show you the samples." He led the way through the living room to French doors that opened to one of her favorite things about the condo, the small outside deck that overlooked the pier and marina. It was a beautiful day, and Mia paused for a moment to admire a sleek thirty-foot sailboat that was gliding toward the marina.

Will handed her the first of several polished pieces of wood. "So, I brought a few options. I think you mentioned that you like some of the darker woods, like Brazilian Cherry?"

Mia nodded. "I do, but I'm glad you brought a few different ones because I really am not sure what would be best."

Will showed her the various wood samples and explained what each was. They were all lovely, but she was drawn to one that was darker with almost a rose tone to it.

"That's the Bolivian Rosewood. It's been popular these past few years."

"I love it. I'll go with that."

Will explained how the process for installing the floors would go, and that he'd order the materials and start once all the cleanup was done. He had a calm, confident way of talking, and it was clear that he loved what he did. Mia knew he'd taken over his grandfather's business after graduating college. His grandfather was ready to retire then, and his father had no interest in the business. Will did all kinds of custom woodwork, too, building entertainment centers and bookcases, even built-in office desks.

"How's business? Is this a busy time for you?" she asked.

"Very. We had a client push off a project, which is how we were able to start on this so soon. We are booked up for months." He grinned. "It's a good problem to have."

"And not surprising. You do beautiful work. How is Caroline? I haven't seen her around in a while."

An uncomfortable expression flashed across Will's face

and he looked away for a moment before answering. "We broke up, actually. She moved off-island yesterday."

Mia's jaw dropped. "I'm so sorry. I had no idea. She moved?"

He sighed. "Things hadn't been great with us for a while. I thought it was maybe just wedding stress, but it was more than that. We both sort of realized that we were getting married just because it was what everyone expected, the logical next step. Not because we were madly in love and eager to spend the rest of our lives together."

"I don't know what to say. I guess it's better to figure that out before the wedding, though, right?"

He nodded. "It is a good thing. Or at least it will be. I'm still getting used to the idea of it. Ultimately, Caroline didn't see herself staying on Nantucket long-term either. She was getting stir-crazy to get off-island, and, well, I can't imagine ever leaving. This is home to me." He looked thoughtful though before adding, "Though I suppose if she was really the one, I would have found a way to make it work somewhere else if it meant being together. It's still nothing like what you went through, though. How are you doing? I still miss Mark. I can't believe it's been a year."

"I know. It seems like it just happened and yet is sort of like another lifetime ago. It's still hard sometimes, but not as hard as it used to be. So that's something."

He smiled, a slow, sympathetic smile, and she knew he understood.

"What are you doing on Sunday?" he asked.

"No plans. Why, what's going on?"

"I'm having a cookout. All the usual suspects will be there." Will and Caroline regularly had people over for cookouts. He had a small house near the beach with a huge deck that was perfect for entertaining.

"I'd love to come. I'll bring some guac and chips or whatever you need?" Mia usually brought her homemade guacamole whenever she and Mark had gone to these kinds of get-togethers. That reminded her she needed to stop and get some avocados, cilantro and lemons to make a batch to bring over to Kate's later.

"Your guac would be perfect. It will be fun."

CHAPTER 6

When Mia arrived at Kate's house a few minutes past seven, she was one of the first ones there. Kate hollered for her to come in when she knocked and Angela was in the kitchen with her, opening a bottle of Bread and Butter chardonnay. Kate was putting a tray of bruschetta in the oven and smiled when she saw Mia.

"Oh, good, you brought your guacamole! Do you want to set it on the kitchen table by the cheese and crackers? Help yourself to wine or a cocktail."

Angela looked up as she finished opening the wine. "Do you like Chardonnay? I could pour you a glass."

"Sure, I'd love some. That's actually one of my favorites." Mia usually drank chardonnay if she was having white wine. Angela poured one for her and then another for Kate.

"Angela brought some amazing cheeses," Kate said.

"What did you say this one is, with the gray line going through it?"

"Humboldt Fog. It's an aged goat cheese. The softer bit near the edge reminds me of Brie."

Mia's stomach rumbled. She hadn't eaten a thing since lunch.

"I've had that one. Izzy brought some home a few days ago. It was amazing."

"How is that going? You're living with your sister now?" Angela asked.

"I was. I'm actually staying at Kate's mother's inn now, though. Insurance covers it and Izzy's house is small, since her boyfriend lives there, too."

"Oh, I bet it's nice to have your own space. Hopefully the renovations won't take too long."

They both turned as the front door opened and Kate's sisters, Kristen and Abby, came in, followed a minute later by their soon-to-be sister-in-law, Beth, who was marrying their younger brother, Chase. Kristen had a platter of brownies. Abby made her famous stuffed mushrooms and Beth brought hummus, pita wedges and an assortment of fresh cut veggies. Kate directed everyone to put the food on the table and while they all helped themselves to wine, she pulled the tray of bubbling bruschetta out of the oven and put them on a large platter.

"Oh, you made your bruschetta! Good, I'm starving," Abby said. "I had one mushroom—for quality control of course, and I had to let Jeff have one."

"Of course," Kate laughed. "How's Natalie? I wasn't sure if you were going to bring her?" Abby's daughter,

Natalie, was almost two and adorable, but into everything.

Abby took a big sip of wine. "No. I told Jeff Mommy needed a break and the two of them could bond."

"Perfect. Okay, everyone help yourselves and grab a seat." Kate brought the platter of bruschetta over, and they all loaded their plates and settled around the big round table. Mia took a little of everything and sighed when she took a bite of the bruschetta. The topping was sweet, creamy and savory over crunchy, garlicky toasted bread.

"Kate, how do you make these? They are so good."

Kate looked pleased by the compliment. "They're easy. It's just Boursin cheese, the packaged stuff you buy at the store. I spread it on toasted, garlic-rubbed baguette slices and top with diced tomatoes that I let sit in some olive oil and balsamic vinegar for about a half hour. I heat them in the oven for maybe ten minutes."

They chatted easily while they ate, and with three of the women engaged, it wasn't long before the conversation turned to wedding planning. Mia didn't bring it up. She didn't think it was appropriate, and she had a sense that Kate was feeling stressed about everything as she hadn't gotten back to her about several things that needed deciding on.

But Mia didn't want to push. They still had time, and she knew that every bride was different and needed to go at their own pace. Some embraced the process more than others. She knew if it was up to Kate that she'd have a much smaller wedding, if a wedding at all. Eloping actually seemed more her style.

"Kate, have you found a dress yet?" Beth asked.

Kate smiled tightly at first, then laughed a moment later. "Not even close. I'll probably have to make a trip off-island soon."

"I found a few options online that you might like. I'll send you an email tomorrow with the store links, and you can get back to me with your thoughts when you have a chance," Mia said. She had an idea now of Kate's taste and had spent an hour or so searching online the night before while she and Penny were relaxing and watching TV.

Kate looked relieved. "Thank you. I'll take a look and let you know ASAP."

"No hurry."

Angela sipped her wine and looked as though she was weighing a decision before finally saying, "Philippe and I were chatting last night, and he suggested I use a wedding planner. We still haven't even set a date yet, and he thought it might make things easier. I'm so busy with work. I just hired two more girls today."

"That's wonderful!" Kate said.

Angela smiled. "We keep getting referrals, which is great. But it doesn't leave me with a lot of free time to plan a wedding. Would you be interested, Mia?"

Mia knew their wedding was likely to be another big one. Angela was new to Nantucket but her fiancé, Philippe, was a celebrity of sorts. Several of his books had been made into movies and TV series so he spent a good deal of time in Los Angeles, and he seemed to know just about everyone on Nantucket and considered them all friends. Angela was easy going and hard-working. Mia knew she would be fun to work with.

"I'd love to. Let me know when you're free to sit down and go over things."

"Maybe next week? Monday mornings I clean the Beach Plum Cove Inn and usually come early to have breakfast with Lisa. We could do it then. I'd love her input, too, if you don't mind?"

"Of course not."

"Mom will love that," Kristen said. "She adores you, and she's in her glory with all these weddings."

"She has a wedding coming up soon too, doesn't she?" Mia asked. She knew Lisa was engaged, but she hadn't mentioned the date.

Kate, Kristen, and Abby all exchanged glances before Kate spoke. "She and Rhett are not on the same page about when to have it or how big. If it was up to Rhett, it would be tomorrow with the whole town invited. Mom doesn't want anything big and fussy, and she doesn't want to overshadow our weddings. Which we, of course, told her was ridiculous."

———

Lisa could tell by the smell that her meatballs were ready to come out of the oven. She opened the oven door and, as suspected, they were perfectly browned. She inhaled deeply as the scent rushed towards her. She'd been trying to cut back on red meat so she hadn't made spaghetti and meatballs in ages. But it was Rhett's favorite dish. She carefully dropped each meatball into the large pot of sauce simmering on the stove, took a small taste of the sauce and added another shake of Italian seasoning, a pinch of sugar and a splash of red wine from the glass she'd just poured. She gave it all a stir, then settled at her kitchen island with her laptop and glass of wine and hopped onto Facebook for a minute to see what her friends were up to.

Thirty minutes later, she heard the front door open, indicating that Rhett was home for the evening. She'd barely touched her wine—she'd been so busy chatting with friends online and was surprised by how quickly the time had passed. Rhett looked surprised and happy when he reached the kitchen.

"Something smells good. You made meatballs? I thought you were off meat. Glad to see you came to your senses," he teased her.

"I'm not off totally, just cutting way back. But I love meatballs, too. Are you starving? Or do you want to have a glass of wine first? We can snack on some cheese and crackers. I got that cheddar you like, the one that has a hint of parmesan."

"I did like that one. Let's do it." Rhett poured himself a glass of wine while Lisa got the cheese and crackers out and set them on the island between them.

"How was the restaurant today? Were you busy?" Lisa asked. Rhett had come to Nantucket when Lisa first opened the inn and decided to stay on indefinitely while he got his newly purchased restaurant ready to open for the season. It had been a hit and even though he owned several other restaurants off-island, he had good managers for those and focused his hands-on attention on the Nantucket one and on Lisa.

"It was a really good day, actually. Our new chef introduced a few items that we are running as specials and if they do well, we'll add them onto the menu. It's early to say for sure, but if the response today is anything to go by, they'll all be on the menu soon."

"Oh, that's fantastic. What are they?" As a foodie, Lisa loved to cook and go out to eat pretty regularly. And since she and Rhett had gotten serious, a solid five pounds had crept onto her, as Rhett enjoyed food as much as she did and that's mostly what they did for their social life, entertain friends or go out to eat. She loved it, but she was trying to make some better choices, which is where eating less red meat came in. But she knew Rhett loved her meatballs, and she had a plan for tonight and wanted him to be in a really good, receptive mood.

"Wasabi crusted tuna with lightly fried avocado wedges and asparagus risotto. Swordfish with a fresh mango salsa, and Caesar salad topped with either fresh lobster meat or grilled scallops."

"I'll have to get in there soon to test them all."

They chatted comfortably over cheese and crackers, and then over meatballs and spaghetti with freshly grated parmesan. Rhett raised his eyebrows when Lisa pulled out the grater and offered him some.

"Wow. We're going all fancy tonight. Sure, load me up."

Lisa grated a fine pile of parmesan over his meatballs and then did the same to hers.

"Save room for dessert. I picked up some Tiramisu from that new Italian bakery. You loved it the last time we had it."

"Have I mentioned how much I love you?" Rhett smiled as he tucked into his pasta and meatballs. When they finished, Lisa added a bit of wine to their glasses and set a generous serving of tiramisu in front of Rhett. After he took his first bite, she took a deep breath and told him what was on her mind.

"So, do you really have your heart set on a big wedding?" She asked.

He paused and set his fork down. "Define big?"

"You've said you want to have a big celebration with everyone we know. Are you okay with just people we really care about?"

"You don't really want a big wedding? I just didn't want you to feel like you couldn't do that. I thought every woman wanted a huge wedding? As long as you're there, I don't honestly care who else shows up," he admitted.

Lisa smiled and relaxed a little. "I've already done that. I don't need a fancy dress and everyone in town at my wedding. What would be perfect would be me in my favorite pink sundress, and you in shorts and that aqua blue golf shirt that you love. And our kids and the minister in the back yard, followed by a cookout. Super casual and beachy. How does that sound to you? It's not very traditional."

Rhett grinned. "Who needs traditional? I'll take comfortable and casual any day. When are you thinking?"

"Well, I had an idea. Your birthday is in two weeks and it's on a Sunday. What if I just tell the kids that we're having a birthday cookout for you and when they all get here, we can surprise them with a wedding, too. That way they don't have to worry about getting us gifts or doing anything else."

"I like it. We don't need a thing. And they have their own weddings to worry about."

"You're sure about this? As long as it's okay with you, I'll go ahead and start planning for it."

Rhett leaned over and kissed her, and she marveled that she still felt butterflies every time he did that. When they pulled apart, he said, "Start the planning. I can't wait to be married to you. Two more weeks is long enough."

CHAPTER 7

Mia was surprised that she hadn't run into Ben yet at breakfast. Saturday morning, while chatting over a blueberry muffin and coffee, Lisa asked if she'd seen him again. As usual, all her girls and even the baby, Natalie, had joined her for Saturday breakfast.

"No, not since I saw him for about two seconds at his family's house. I think he is mostly out late and sleeps in."

Lisa nodded. "If he makes it to breakfast, it's usually about five or ten minutes before ten."

Kate looked intrigued. "Who is Ben?"

"He's Mia's next-door neighbor. About the same age, I'd guess. Very handsome."

"Is he single?" Abby asked.

"I think he might be. I thought he could be a good candidate, if Mia was ready to start dating?"

Mia shook her head and automatically said, "I'm not ready." She wondered if she ever would be. Dating just wasn't something she thought about these days. It didn't feel right, not when she still often felt so sad about Mark.

Lisa reached out and gave her hand a squeeze. "You'll know when it's the right time. And when you do, be sure to let us know so we can keep an eye out for you."

Mia relaxed and smiled, grateful that Lisa understood and didn't push. "Thank you. I'll do that."

"So, Kristen, what's new with you?" Lisa asked.

"I have some news. I just heard back from Andrew at the gallery, and I have a show there in a few weeks, on the Friday night of Memorial Day weekend, and the paintings will stay up after that, until they sell." Kristen was a local artist, and Mia had one of her paintings in her condo. It had quite a bit of damage, though, and Will was doubtful that it could be restored.

"Oh, that's great, honey," Lisa said. "I'll make sure Rhett knows to keep that night free."

"Izzy and I will make sure to come by, too," Mia added.

"How's Tyler doing?" Abby asked.

"He's really good. He's halfway through his newest book now, so it's going much easier. He said he might even be done two weeks before his deadline, which would be a first." Tyler was a famous mystery writer and he and Kristen lived next to each other, in matching cottages. Mia knew that Tyler had gone through a rough period after his mother died unexpectedly, and he had relapsed and started drinking again. He got the help he needed, though, and it seemed like he was back on the wagon and things were going really well with him and Kristen.

"Are you all going to Will's cookout on Sunday?" Kate asked.

"I'll be there," Mia said.

"Tyler and I are planning to go." Kristen took a sip of her coffee and reached for a bite of the muffin that was mostly untouched on her plate. Mia didn't think she'd ever seen Kristen finish anything. There wasn't a crumb left on Mia's plate.

"Jeff and I are going to his mother's for dinner, so we'll miss it. It will be strange without Caroline there. I was so surprised to hear they broke up," Abby said.

"I always thought he was too nice for her," Kate said. "I'm not surprised that she moved off-island."

Mia nodded. "I know what you mean. I liked Caroline, but I think Will would be better with someone a little more laid-back."

Kate glanced at her sisters and smiled. "I couldn't agree more. Do you know of anyone for him?"

Mia was surprised by the question. "No. They just broke up. I doubt he's ready to start dating again."

"You might be surprised. Guys often rebound faster, it seems," Kate said.

"Jeff's friend Michael broke up with his girlfriend of seven years and less than three months later, he was engaged to someone else," Abby added.

Mia didn't see that happening with Will, but she didn't say anything. When they all finished eating and went their separate ways, Mia went upstairs. She was going to take Penny for a walk on the beach. She'd taken her out quickly to do her business before breakfast but didn't have enough time earlier for her usual walk.

Penny was all excited when Mia returned to the room and said the magic words, "Want to go outside?" The little dog jumped around, wagging her tail and moving so much that Mia had to grab hold of her to get her leash on. Once they were ready, she pulled on a lightweight jacket and opened the door to head out. She'd just locked the door behind her when Ben came out of his room and stopped short when he saw her. He was wearing sweat-pants and sneakers, and nodded at the leash.

"Are you two going out for a walk? I was just heading out for one, too. Mind if I join you?"

Mia was surprised that he'd want to, but nodded and said, "Of course. We were going to walk down the beach and back."

"Perfect. Lead the way."

Ben followed them down the stairs, and they all walked to the beach, which was just a few steps past the back yard. A well-worn path led down to the water's edge. They walked along the sandy part that was packed down and firm. Now and then Penny tried to pull them closer toward the water so she could dip her toes and nose in. Ben peppered her with questions as they walked, asking her about her family and when she was last in the city.

"It's been a little over a year. I went there for a few weeks right after Mark died, but I haven't been back since. That's not really my world anymore."

Ben looked at her curiously. "I heard about that. I'm sorry." He was quiet for a moment before asking, "You're really here full-time now? You don't think you'd ever want to go back?"

She nodded. "This is my home now. I love it here."

"Oh, I love it, too. I bought that condo so I can come here whenever I want, but I doubt I'll be here much, if at all, in the winter. Seems like it would be way too quiet for me."

"It would be," Mia assured him. "If you love the hustle and bustle of summer and of Manhattan every day, you might go stir-crazy here in the winter."

He smiled. "Not you, though?"

"No."

"So, you're a wedding planner? Bethany and my mom only hire the best, so you must be good."

Mia was pleased by the compliment. "I hope so. I try. What do you do?"

"Real estate investing and an online course on how to do it. I do most of the property purchasing and development in Manhattan and in the summer focus more on my online course business. That's easy to do from anywhere."

"That sounds interesting. I've always been fascinated by real estate," Mia admitted. She and Izzy often talked about how fun it would be to do a flip together, to find an underpriced property and fix it up. Though neither one of them had any construction experience and Nantucket wasn't a good place to find real estate bargains, and they didn't have the money to do it. But whenever they watched one of those flipping shows on TV, they always thought it looked fun.

"Real estate is great. Do you do any investing?"

"No. I bought my condo a few years ago, and that's about it. Do you flip properties?"

He nodded. "Sometimes, yeah. But lately, I've been more into buying rental properties, which generate a steady income."

They chatted a bit more about real estate and the various restaurants they both liked. By the time they got back to the inn, Ben said he was starving.

"I really need to get up earlier. I'm going to take a drive into town and grab a bite. I don't suppose you're hungry yet?"

Mia laughed. "No, I just ate."

"Right. Well, enjoy the rest of your day. Anytime you want company for a walk, let me know. If I'm around, I'll gladly join you.

"Thanks, Ben. I'll keep that in mind. See you soon."

AFTER GOING TO KATE'S APPETIZER PARTY THE NIGHT before and with Will's cookout coming up on Sunday, Mia didn't mind at all that she found herself without any plans on a Saturday night. She stopped by the grocery store and stocked up on some junk food—potato chips and her favorite Cherry Garcia frozen yogurt. She had a couple of good books that she'd been meaning to dive into, and she knew that Penny certainly would welcome her company for the evening. Her only plans were to maybe get some takeout, then head back to her room and hunker down.

But as she was driving home from the grocery store, her cell phone rang, and she was surprised to see that it was Izzy. Surprised because they had already spoken earlier in the day. They usually talked most days, even if it was just a quick call to catch up.

"Hey, Mia. I'm not catching you in the middle of anything, am I?"

Mia laughed. "No, I'm just out grocery shopping. Nothing too exciting. What's up?"

"Well, I know it's kind of short notice—you probably already have plans tonight?"

"No plans. I was actually going to stay in. Why, what are you up to?"

"Just wondered if you felt like doing something? Maybe having a girls' night sleepover, like we talked about?"

Something in Izzy's voice sounded a bit off.

"Sure, I'd love to." Mia paused for a moment before asking, "Is everything okay?"

"Everything's fine." There was a moment of silence followed by a heavy sigh. "Rick got some bad news yesterday at work, and he's not taking it well. I thought I'd give him a break and get out of his hair for the night."

"Okay. Well, I'm heading home now. So, come on over anytime."

"Thanks, Mia. I'll see you in about an hour."

MIA STOPPED AT BRADFORD'S LIQUORS ON THE WAY HOME

to pick up a bottle of Izzy's favorite wine. She had a feeling that they were going to need it.

An hour later, Izzy arrived with her overnight bag and a bottle of wine as well. She gave Mia a hug, set her bag down, and handed her sister the wine. It was Josh Cabernet, Mia's favorite red.

"Oh, this is so nice!" Izzy looked around the room, walked over to a window and took in the view. It was a sunny day, and the tide was coming in. Mia had the window open a few inches to let in the crisp air. The sea was calm, and the sound of the waves was soothing.

"Thanks. We are liking it here." Penny ran over to Izzy, wagging her tail and barking to get her attention. Izzy laughed as she bent over, scooped the small dog up and gave her a hug.

"I've missed you, Penny!" Izzy put her down after a moment, then sat on the edge of Mia's bed and Penny jumped up next to her.

"So, what do you feel like doing?" Mia asked. "We could grab a bite somewhere or we could stay in, but all I have is potato chips, ice cream and wine."

Izzy laughed nervously. "I wouldn't mind going out somewhere casual. Millie's, maybe? It's early enough that we shouldn't have to wait too long, and then we can come back here and relax."

"I'm always up for Millie's. That sounds great." Mia sensed that Izzy wasn't ready to talk yet but, after some guac and chips and a drink, she might be. They took Penny out for a quick walk and fed her before heading over to Millie's.

The restaurant wasn't crowded yet, as predicted, so they went upstairs to the bar area and sat at one of the high-top tables. They were tempted to get margaritas, but since they had wine for later, they both decided to stay with red wine. They also put in an order for shrimp, and scallop and bacon tacos and some guacamole and chips to share.

They chatted about unimportant things while they ate and sipped their wine.

"We had a good day at the store today. It was really busy. I'm not sure why."

"I thought it seemed busier downtown when I was out and about earlier," Mia said.

"Right. Memorial Day weekend isn't far off. Seems like it gets busy earlier every year."

After a while, Mia grew tired of talking about nothing. She finally asked the uncomfortable question that had to be asked. "So, what's going on with Rick?"

Izzy sighed, then fiddled with a tortilla chip, taking her time getting the perfect amount of guacamole onto it. Finally, she spoke. "It's been kind of hard lately." She reached for another chip and Mia waited for her to continue. "So, his new job wasn't working out, kind of like the last one. They laid him off at the end of the day yesterday. And he's—he's not taking it well."

"What did he do?" Mia wasn't liking the sound of this at all.

"I never really saw this side of him until we moved in together. He gets frustrated and angry so fast. Lately, I've felt like I've had to walk on eggshells around him because

I never know what's going to set him off. His moods change so quickly. But last night was the worst I've seen yet. He actually threw a chair through the kitchen window. I think it freaked both of us out."

"Did he touch you?" Mia asked.

Izzy shook her head. "No. He just lost his temper, really lost it. But the window was the only thing that was damaged."

This time. "Why didn't you call me last night? You could've come here then."

"I didn't feel like I was in any danger. I know that Rick would never actually hurt me. He was just upset. He apologized immediately and was as sweet as could be afterwards. He felt terrible. He went to the hardware store first thing this morning and fixed the window. So, it's as good as new."

"So...if everything's fine, why are you here tonight?"

Izzy took a big sip of wine before answering. "Rick went to lunch with some friends and they had a few beers. He had more than a few. When he came home, I could tell he was drunk, and in a mood, and I just didn't want to deal. I told him that you and I already had plans and I had forgotten to tell him. He was half asleep in his chair in front of the TV when I left."

"So, what are you going to do about this? He's lost two jobs recently. Do you think things are going to get better? I'm worried for you."

"I'm not ready to give up on him yet. I really do love him. He's had a hard time of it lately, and I want to see what I can do to support him and to help make things better. I just really needed a break." Izzy smiled and reached for yet another chip. "And I wanted to spend some time with my sister, like we talked about."

Mia wanted to tell her sister that she thought she was crazy and that Rick was a loser and potentially dangerous, but she knew her sister wasn't ready to hear it. Not yet.

After they finished eating, they went back to Mia's place and took Penny out for a walk on the beach. They all needed the exercise and fresh air.

Once they were inside and settled for the night, Mia opened one of the bottles of wine. They each had another glass and after a while broke out the chips and ice cream and stayed up late watching a marathon of Meg Ryan movies on Netflix.

The next morning, after walking Penny, they went for coffee downstairs and were planning to go out for breakfast, but Lisa talked them into eating her special lobster quiche instead.

"I don't make this one often, and Izzy is your guest which means she's more than welcome to have breakfast, too. You just missed the girls. They were here earlier. I'll leave the two of you to enjoy your food."

When she disappeared into the main house, Mia explained that Lisa's girls usually joined her for breakfast on Saturdays. "We'll see them tomorrow. They'll all be at Will's cookout, except for Abby. You and Rick are going, right?"

"I'm not sure if he's still going to want to go. I hope so."

"Well, if he doesn't, you can go with me. It should be fun."

"We'll see." They both looked up as Ben walked into the room and went straight for the food.

"Isn't that your neighbor?" Izzy spoke softly. "I'd recognize Ben Billings anywhere. He's even better looking now that he's older, if that's possible."

Mia nodded. "I agree. I didn't place him immediately when I first saw him, but it was late at night and I'd just woken up."

Ben loaded his plate with quiche and after adding a half dozen or so sugars to his coffee, he saw Mia and walked over to their table.

"We're finally here at the same time. Mind if I join you?

"Of course. You remember my sister, Izzy?"

Ben sat and smiled at Izzy. "Of course. You always had that long hair. Are you just visiting, or do you live here, too?"

"I live here, too. I run a shop down by the pier."

He nodded. "That's where my condo is, by Mia's. I'm hoping it won't be too long before the work is done and we can move in. I met with Will, the guy doing the restoration, yesterday and he seemed to think it might not take as long as they originally thought. Maybe just a few more weeks."

"Oh, that's great news," Izzy said.

"I saw him this week, too," Mia added. "I picked out new hardwood flooring. I can't wait to see what it looks like once it's in."

"I was a little freaked out when this happened. I was set to move in the next week. I was afraid I'd made a huge mistake by buying this condo. But Will assured me that when it's done, it will be like brand new."

"Will's a good friend. You don't have anything to worry about. He does beautiful work. He makes furniture, too. He was actually making me an entertainment center before the fire happened, so I'll have that when it's all done, too."

"No kidding. I might have to talk to him about that. I still need to fully furnish my place."

They chatted a few more minutes until Ben was finished eating, then said their goodbyes. Ben left to go fishing with a friend while Mia and Izzy went back to the room to get Izzy's bag. Mia walked her out to her car and hugged her goodbye.

"Call me later. Let me know if you want me to pick you up for the cookout."

"I will. Thanks, Mia. It was good to get away for the night. This was fun."

"It was. And you know you're welcome anytime."

CHAPTER 8

K ate kissed Jack goodbye as she headed toward the door Sunday morning. She had fifteen minutes to meet Sam at The Bean, and it took ten minutes to get there, so she should be fine.

"Don't forget, we have Will's cookout later. We should head over around four."

"Got it. Have fun on your coffee date," Jack teased her.

"Very funny. I'll be home in about an hour."

Jack was being pretty understanding, considering that she was meeting a former boyfriend for coffee. But she assured him it was just meeting an old friend who was married with kids. Plus, Sam knew she was engaged. Kate knew not all guys would be as calm. And truth be told, Kate knew she wouldn't be thrilled if one of Jack's old girlfriends surfaced and wanted to meet up after not seeing him in years. She wasn't sure she would have been as understanding as Jack.

When she arrived at The Bean, it wasn't too busy. She looked around and then she saw him—the tall, familiar figure with the thick, blonde hair that he always wore a little on the long side. Sam smiled when he saw her and stood. He was a little fuller than she last remembered, and he had some fine laugh lines now around his mouth and eyes, but they looked good on him.

"Kate! You haven't changed a bit. You look great."

"It's good to see you, Sam. You look the same, too."

They both moved towards each other at the same time for a quick hug.

"What do you want to drink? I'll get our coffees," he asked.

"Just black for me."

"Save our seats. I'll be right back."

Kate settled at the small table by a window where Sam had been waiting. In just a few minutes, he was back with two paper cups of coffee and handed one to her.

"So, fill me in on everything. You're living on Nantucket year-round now?"

Kate launched into what she'd been up to since college, living in Boston, working at Boston Style magazine until it was sold and she was laid off. Then moving home to Nantucket, writing and publishing her first mystery, doing some freelance magazine work and falling in love with Jack.

"And so, we got engaged. I'm planning the wedding now."

"Congratulations. How's that coming along?"

Kate made a face. "Truthfully, I hate every minute of

it, and I even have a wonderful wedding planner helping. I've just never been a big wedding kind of girl."

"No, you never were," he agreed. "I'm sure once everything is decided and the big day comes, you'll have a blast."

Kate grinned. "You're probably right. I wish I could skip ahead to that day. But enough about me. What have you been up to? You mentioned that you married and had kids. Tell me about them, and about your wife, how did you meet?"

Sam took a deep breath and his smile faded. Kate leaned forward, sensing suddenly that this might not be a happy story.

"I met Mary in college, sophomore year, and that was kind of it for both of us. We both fell hard fast and knew we didn't want to date anyone else, ever. We got married six months after graduating. And everything was great for ten years. Except that we couldn't seem to get pregnant. We tried everything. Finally, when we came to terms that it just wasn't going to happen for us, Mary suddenly found herself pregnant—and with twins. The doctor said that happens sometimes, when you stop trying and just relax."

"Wow, and twins. Did you have more after that?"

Sam shook his head slowly and Kate was immediately sorry she'd asked the question.

"No, just the girls, Becky and Sarah. They're seven now. A few years after they were born, Mary found a lump and was diagnosed with stage three breast cancer. We thought we could beat it. She did great for a few years, but a little over a year ago she had a bad cough, like a bronchitis that she couldn't shake. They did a chest x-ray, and that's when we learned that it had spread to her lungs and her liver. She died five months later."

"Oh, Sam, I'm so sorry. How are you and the kids coping?"

"It's been hard, for all of us. I took the kids to a therapist that was recommended, and I think that was a good idea. We just try to focus on all the happy memories. Send balloons up for her on holidays, that kind of thing. It's a lot for kids that age."

"For any age," Kate said.

He smiled. "Right. Anyway, it's been a hard year, to put it mildly, and I've wanted to keep things as stable and smooth for the girls as possible. I'm a consultant, and I stopped traveling. I do everything remotely now over the phone and online using email or Zoom for video calls or presentations. But it's been a lot. I'm basically home with the girls 24/7 and I love them, but I was feeling burned out. My mother has been after me to move home for years. I finally agreed that it was a good idea and so far, it's been great. The girls get to see their grandparents more and my mother loves to babysit, which gives me a break."

"How are your parents?" Kate had always really like them. Lucy was an extrovert, involved in all kinds of local clubs and charities, while his father was the quiet one. He was a kind, friendly man and worked as a tax and estate attorney.

"They're great. They said to tell you hello. My

mother pushed me to join a local bereavement group for people that had lost spouses or partners. I was against the idea at first. But, as usual, she was right. Everyone there knows what I'm going through, and it's been helpful to talk about it with them."

"Oh, that's great. I didn't know there was a group like that here." An idea came to Kate, of someone else who could benefit from it. "A good friend lost her fiancé a year ago, and I know she has been struggling, though she puts up a good front. I'd like to tell her about the group."

"Sure, I'll message you the details."

"So, when did you get back? Are the girls settling in? Tell me about them? Do they look alike?" The questions rushed out and Kate laughed. "Sorry to bombard you, it's the former reporter in me."

But Sam didn't seem to mind. "A little over a month ago. The girls seem to love it. My parents are, of course, spoiling them rotten. And we're staying in their rental property, a year-round cottage that is just a short walk away, so they run over there all the time. They actually look nothing alike. You almost wouldn't even guess that they are sisters. People say that Becky looks more like me, same color hair and eyes. She's bubbly and full of energy. Sarah takes after her mom, darker hair, same smile and she's more quiet, introspective. She worries about me, is more of a nurturer. It's cute."

"They sound adorable. I'd love to meet them sometime. Jack and I usually have a cookout over Memorial Day weekend. You'll have to come by then if you're free."

"We'd love to and thanks for the invite. I wanted to

reach out to you sooner, but I worried that it might not be welcome, or that your fiancé would mind."

"Jack is pretty understanding. I'd love for you to meet him." She thought for a moment. "When you're ready to start dating, let me know. I could introduce you to some people."

Sam shook his head. "Thanks, but dating isn't on my radar at all. I can't imagine when it will be." He paused and then his voice cracked a little. "I still think about Mary every day."

"Of course, you do. I'm really sorry, Sam. I wish I could do something to help."

"Just meeting me today helped. It has gotten easier as everyone said that it would. Moving home here was the best decision, though. We'll definitely plan to come for your Memorial Day weekend cookout. I was thinking to take the girls down to the pier that day, too, to show them the Figawi madness with all the boats coming in."

"That's a great idea. They'll love it." Memorial Day weekend was like the unofficial kickoff to the summer season on Nantucket, and the Figawi race was impressive to see. Several hundred sailboats of all sizes raced from Hyannis to Nantucket and spent the weekend on the island before sailing back on Monday.

Sam glanced at his watch. "I wish I could stay longer, but I have to get back to take the kids to their dance lessons."

Kate stood. "It was really great seeing you, Sam. I'm glad you're back here."

"Me, too. And I'll send you that info later today for your friend."

THE GIRLS WERE WAITING FOR HIM ON THE FRONT PORCH. Sarah was sitting next to his mother on the big sofa swing, brushing his mother's hair while Becky was chattering non-stop and doing pirouettes while she spoke. As soon as he pulled in the driveway, she stopped mid-twirl and came running to greet him.

"Daddy, you're late! We have to leave now."

"We're not going to be late. Go grab your bag and let's go."

"You are cutting it awfully close," his mother said. "Did you have a nice time, at least?

He smiled. "Yes, it was nice to see Kate and catch up. I'll fill you in when I get home. Come on, girls."

"Who did you go see, Daddy?" Sarah asked once they were on the way.

"An old friend. Her name is Kate, and she invited us to her house for a cookout Memorial Day weekend."

Sarah thought about that for a moment. "Will there be hot dogs?" she asked seriously.

"I don't know for sure, but there's a very good chance. Probably hamburgers, too."

Sarah nodded. "That's okay, then. We'll go."

"You're taking us to see the sailboats still, right?" Becky sounded worried.

"Yes, of course, honey." He pulled up to the dance

studio and made sure the girls had everything they needed. He watched them run inside and then headed back to his mother's. He had an hour to kill before he had to pick up the girls. His mother was in the kitchen, dicing celery and onions for a pot of chicken soup. She looked up when she saw him.

"Have a cup of tea with me?"

"Sure."

She added the cut veggies and a chicken to the pot of simmering water. Then washed her hands thoroughly with soap and water before making their tea. Once it was ready, she brought the two cups to the kitchen table and sat down.

"So, tell me about Kate. I heard something about an engagement, but maybe that's not true?

He laughed. He knew his mother was hoping it wasn't true. She had always really liked Kate. "It's true, and she seems very happy."

"Oh, that's too bad. I mean, I'm happy for her. I just thought it would be nice if the two of you got back together."

"I didn't go see her with that intention. I'm really not ready to date anyone. Not yet."

"It's been over a year, honey. It might be good for you to get out there and meet some people."

Sam groaned. "Mom, seriously I have no desire to get back 'out there'. I'll let you know when I do."

His mother sighed and changed the subject. "Okay, so you'll all stay for supper tonight? I made some fresh bread this morning and the chicken soup will be ready by the time you get home with the girls. And I got a blueberry pie at the market. The girls love that. Your father should be home by then, too. He's off fishing."

"Sure, Mom. We'll stay for dinner." He knew his mother just worried about him and wanted to see him happy again. And he was happy. He had the girls, and they were his whole world. It was nice to see Kate again, and hopefully reconnect with some more friends he once knew and make some new ones. He was looking forward to going to Kate's cookout. He thought that would be fun for the girls, too. A glance at the clock told him it was just about time to go get them.

"We'll be back in a bit and I'm sure the girls will love to stay for dinner."

CHAPTER 9

"I can't wait until our fiftieth wedding anniversary. We'll be one of those annoyingly happy couples that are still madly in love…"

Mia's eyes welled up as she remembered Mark's words. They'd been eating ice cream together on a rainy Sunday, and he'd been a good sport and watched *When Harry Met Sally* with her. One of her favorite movies, she'd lost count of how many times she'd seen it. She'd always loved the interviews with the old married couples throughout the movie. She hadn't watched it since Mark died, and just a few seconds of the commercial telling her that it was going to be on later that week triggered the memory, and the tears.

Mia clicked off the TV and checked the time. It was a little after two. She'd been lazily watching an old Marilyn Monroe movie while she ate some microwave popcorn instead of lunch. Will's cookout was later that afternoon and knew she'd want to eat everything.

Penny looked concerned. She'd seen the tears and always knew when Mia was feeling sad. Instead of hopping around the room like she usually did, she rubbed against Mia's knee and looked up at her as if asking how she could help. Mia thought for a moment and decided that they had time for a walk on the beach to de-stress.

"Want to go outside?" She knew it would be good for both of them.

They took a longer walk than usual and were gone for just over an hour. Mia was about to jump in the shower and start getting ready when her phone rang and it was Izzy.

"Hey, there."

"Rick doesn't want to go to the cookout. He's glued to the TV watching golf. Do you mind picking me up?"

"I'll be over at a quarter to four."

MIA PULLED UP AT IZZY'S AT TEN OF FOUR. SHE JUST wasn't moving as fast as she'd hoped. She couldn't decide what to wear, and then what she settled on needed to be ironed. And it was silly because there was no one she was looking to impress. She was just having a hard time lately making any decisions. It had been like that since Mark died, especially if she was having a bad day. Some days were much better than others, and overall, she felt a little less sad as each week passed. But sometimes all the feelings came rushing back, always when she least expected it.

She was about to get out of the car and go get Izzy when the front door opened, and her sister came out carrying a bakery box and a bottle of wine. She looked amazing, as usual. Mia always admired her sister's sense of style. She could put anything on, and it would look good. Today she was wearing two tank tops, a sheer yellow long and floaty one layered over a simple white one, and wide white linen pants and gold sandals. Her hair was down, long and curly, the tousled blonde beach look that Mia could never achieve and gave up trying.

She'd instead blown her hair straight, and wore her best jeans and a blue and white striped boatneck top and pale pink Sperry boat shoes. Izzy climbed into the passenger seat and Mia pulled out of the driveway.

At a few minutes past four, they reached Will's house. He lived on a corner lot and there was plenty of room along the street for parking. There was already a good crowd gathered. Kate and Jack were sitting at one of Will's picnic tables, and Kristen and Tyler were opening bottles of diet soda as Mia and Izzy walked onto Will's back deck. Mia knew Kristen often had soda instead of a drink when she was out with Tyler. Will walked over to give them a welcome hug.

"I'm so glad you both came. Help yourself to whatever you want to drink. There's wine, beer, soda and mixers on the table by Kristen."

"Where would you like me to put this?" Mia held up her guacamole.

Will's eyes lit up. "You made your guac!"

She grinned. "Of course, I did."

"I'd say leave it here with me, but you should probably set it on the big picnic table where Kate is sitting." He glanced at the bakery box Izzy was carrying. "What's that?"

"Cannoli from the new Italian bakery."

"Awesome. Maybe set those in the kitchen for now, so they stay cool till later."

"Do you have a bowl I could use for the tortilla chips?" Mia asked.

"In the kitchen cupboard, the one closest to the refrigerator."

They both went inside. Izzy dropped off the cannoli, while Mia poured the chips into a big bowl. They stopped at the drinks table on the deck to pour a glass of wine each and joined Kate and Jack at the big table. Mia set the guac and chips in the middle next to a plate of cheese and crackers that she guessed Kate brought. Jack wandered off to chat with Will, and Izzy saw a friend and went to say hello. So, for a few minutes it was just Kate and Mia.

"This is dangerous, having this all to ourselves," Kate said as she reached for a chip and loaded it with guacamole. Mia helped herself to the cheese and crackers.

"Will's making his famous Juicy Lucy burgers, too. So, I probably shouldn't eat too much of this cheese." Will's burgers were the best. He seasoned the meat with a little Worcestershire, garlic, salt and pepper, and stacked two patties with American cheese in the middle.

"Those are good," Kate agreed. "But I'm having

some cheese, too." They snacked for a few minutes and chatted about her friend Sam that had just recently moved back to the island.

"I lost touch with him when we both went off to college. He never came back after graduating. Instead, he got married and settled down. He's back now, though, with his twin daughters, but unfortunately he lost his wife about a year ago."

"Oh, no, how awful for him." Mia's heart went out to Kate's friend that she didn't even know. As hard as it had been for Mia, at least they didn't have any kids yet. That seemed like it would be harder, for all of them.

Kate explained how long it had taken them to get pregnant and then how his wife Mary got sick. Mia wondered sometimes, as awful as it had been to lose Mark, if it might have been worse to know he was going to die and be helpless to stop it from happening. It was awful either way.

"So, anyway, Sam was telling me about this bereavement group his mother made him go to. He said it's been really helpful. I didn't realize there was a group like that here, did you?"

Mia nodded. "Yeah. Izzy tried to get me to go when Mark first died. I never did, though." The idea of it had seemed intimidating at the time, to join a group full of strangers. Mia imagined they were mostly older people that she wouldn't have anything in common with.

"Sam said he wasn't too keen on the idea, either, but his mother pushed him. And he said it's been great to talk about what he's going through with people that understand. He said it's all ages, too. I think you should go."

Mia shook her head. "I don't know. It's probably too late now."

Kate took a slip of paper and handed it to Mia. It had the name of the group, time they met, address and phone number.

"The phone number is only if you have questions. It's open to all and you can just show up. And it's not too late. Sam's wife passed a month before Mark did. You might be a good friend for him. He doesn't know many people here."

Mia frowned. "You're not trying to play matchmaker; are you? I thought you said Sam grew up here?"

Kate laughed. "I'm not. At all, I swear. I just thought it might be good for you to have people to talk to that understand. And Sam did grow up here, but he's been away for years. I'm one of the few people left here that he knows. Anyway, just think about it. You don't have to decide now."

"Okay, I'll think about it. Thanks for thinking of me."

Angela and Izzy joined them at the table a few minutes later and before they knew it, Will was hollering for everyone to come and get their burgers. They were as good as Mia remembered, and it was a fun few hours.

A bit later, she went to get more wine and stopped to chat with Will as he set out Izzy's cannoli. Kristen brought peanut butter chocolate chip cookies for dessert, too, and Angela had made a cheesecake. Mia and Will both grabbed a cannoli and ate them as they leaned against the deck railing.

"Your burgers were awesome as usual. Where did you learn to make them like that?"

"My mom was from Minneapolis and she always made them that way. She said that's where it started."

"Oh, heads up, I told my neighbor, Ben, that you make furniture. He seemed really interested, so he might be in touch. He bought the unit next to mine."

Will grinned. "Thanks. He's already called and might have me build out his office. Since I'm doing the restoration anyway, I can just work that in. It's going to be a cool project. He said he wants everything—desk, cabinets, bookcases, the works."

"Oh, that's wonderful. I'm sure it will be beautiful."

Izzy walked up and put a few cannoli on a paper plate. "They're not all for me. I'm bringing one for Angela, Kate and Kristen."

"Sure, you are," Will teased her.

Izzy laughed. "I'll catch up with you two later." She wandered off to deliver the desserts, and Mia saw that Will watched her with a concerned expression.

"Is everything okay with your sister?"

"What do you mean?"

"I was chatting with her a bit earlier, and she's not her usually bubbly self, just quieter than usual. And that guy Rick isn't with her. Did they break up?"

"No, unfortunately not," Mia said impulsively.

"I take it you're not a fan?"

"No. I'm not. I stayed with them for a few days right

after the fire and—well, it was a long few days. She wants to try to make things work, though, so I'm not saying anything. For now."

"Yeah, people don't want to hear it, even when they know better."

One of Will's friends walked over and after chatting with him for a few minutes, Mia excused herself to go back to where the girls were sitting. She joined them and they were having a great time until Izzy reached into her purse and pulled out her cell phone to check the time. Her face immediately lost its color.

"What's wrong?" Mia asked.

Izzy sighed. "It's nothing. I had my ringer off and missed a bunch of calls and text messages from Rick, wondering when I'm coming home. I'd better call him and see what he wants."

She called him, and her face grew tense as she listened. Rick was talking loudly but Mia couldn't make out what he was saying.

"I don't know what time I'm coming home. I'm not driving. You know everyone here. It's the same people we always see." She paused and rolled her eyes at Mia as Rick continued to talk. "Rick, you're being ridiculous. I'll be home in a little while. Goodbye."

She hung up and put the phone back in her purse.

"What was that all about?" Mia asked. Izzy still looked annoyed.

"I don't know what his problem is. He was going on and on about wanting to know who was here and said he heard I was meeting some guy here. Which is absurd."

"Why would he think that?"

"I have no idea. He's been weird like that lately. He wants to know where I am at all times, when I'll be home and who I'm with. It's like he doesn't trust me or thinks other guys are trying to date me."

"Was he like this before you moved in with him?"

"No. He was a perfect gentleman, and crazy about me. It's a little much now. He needs to chill. But, maybe we should get going soon, if you're ready?"

Mia nodded. The party was winding down, and she was full and tired.

"Sure, let's head out."

———

MIA DROPPED IZZY OFF AND AN HOUR LATER TEXTED HER.

"Everything okay there?" Izzy's phone call earlier with Rick was unsettling, and Mia wanted to make sure her sister was all right.

A few seconds later, Izzy replied, "All good here. Rick said he just missed me."

The words were reassuring, but Mia couldn't help but wonder, for the first time, if her sister was telling the whole truth.

CHAPTER 10

Angela and Lisa were already sitting at a table when Mia joined them for breakfast the next day. Lisa had a plate of what looked like scrambled eggs with peppers, onions and cheese and a piece of toast, and Angela had a small scoop of eggs and a big slice of some kind of coffee cake.

"That's Angela's favorite," Lisa said with a smile. "Cinnamon walnut coffee cake with sour cream. You have to try it."

Mia went for the eggs, but instead of her usual toast, she cut a sliver of the coffee cake, poured a mug of hot coffee and joined them. After one bite of the coffee cake, she almost wished she'd cut a bigger slice. Lisa seemed to read her mind.

"You can always go back for more."

Mia laughed. "I'm going to gain weight living here!"

They chatted about the cookout and what they had going on for the week, while they ate. Once they finished and cleared their dishes away, Mia and Angela went for more coffee, then settled down to discuss what Angela envisioned for her wedding. Mia took notes as Angela talked.

"So, Philippe, as you probably have guessed, wants a big wedding. Sky's the limit, really. He doesn't care what it costs. He just wants all of his friends and family there." She paused a moment and pulled out a spreadsheet that she'd printed off her computer and handed it to Mia. "That's the guest list so far."

Mia glanced at the spreadsheet and her jaw dropped as she saw the final number at the bottom.

"Six hundred and fifty?" It would be the biggest wedding she'd ever coordinated.

Angela nodded. "So far. Every day, he thinks of someone else. Everyone he's ever met is apparently a good friend." She grinned. "I love him, but our wedding is going to be ridiculously lopsided. My guest list has maybe a dozen people, and most of them are already his friends, too." Mia knew Angela didn't have any family left and that her closest friend lived in San Francisco.

"I assume Jane is on the list?"

Angela smiled. "Yes, she's my maid of honor. She's never been to Nantucket, so they are going to make a vacation of it and stay for a week or so."

"That will be nice for you both," Lisa said.

"I can't wait to show her around," Angela agreed.

Mia took a moment and looked through the list. She recognized about half of the names.

"It looks like about half of the guest list will be coming from off-island, so they'll all need hotel rooms?"

"Philippe suggested we just give them a few names of places to stay and let them make their own arrangements." That was what Mia would have suggested, too.

"Perfect. I can put a list together. Have you thought about where you want to have it? Catered, of course." There wasn't a restaurant on Nantucket big enough to accommodate a wedding that size.

"Yes, definitely catered. We were actually thinking we'd like to have it here, a buffet on the beach, maybe. Something fun and casual, with tents in case it rains and dancing after. One of Philippe's friends has a band, and he said they want to play."

Mia pictured their property. Philippe had a gorgeous, custom built home on the water. His backyard that faced the ocean was huge and there was plenty of room on the beach for tents, tables and chairs. Angela considered the logistics of getting hundreds of chairs and everything else there and knew she'd be hiring a team to help. She had some regular people that she called on when she needed extra hands to help set up a wedding. The caterers took care of making sure there were enough servers and they handled their own setup and cleanup. Mia would be overseeing everything, so that Angela could just relax and enjoy her wedding.

"Have you thought about your wedding dress?"

Angela picked up her iPad and pulled up her email. She found what she was looking for, clicked to a website and turned it around to show Mia.

"I found that last night, from JCrew. It's kind of exactly what I had in mind, so I went ahead and ordered it in two sizes. If one of them fits and it looks good, I'll just return the other. But, I'm a little skeptical that it can be this easy. It was even on sale!"

Mia looked at the simple but elegant ivory slip dress. It had spaghetti straps, and she thought it might look lovely on Angela. It reminded her of the sleek dress that Carolyn Kennedy had worn.

"That's beautiful. And I'll keep my fingers crossed that it works for you. How wonderful would that be to knock it off your list so easily?"

"I know, right?"

"That really is gorgeous, Angela," Lisa added.

They chatted a while longer, going over possible menu ideas. Angela was leaning toward an Italian theme. "Philippe said he doesn't care what we do for food and that I should pick out whatever I like."

"Do you have any thoughts on who you might want to use for catering? I have a list of people I often use."

"I do, actually. I'd love to see if Mimi's Place can do it. We were in there last week for dinner and I was chatting with Mandy and Emma at the bar while we were waiting for our table. They said they've been doing quite a few weddings. They mostly do them in the restaurant, but she said they have been doing catering, too."

"Oh, that's a great idea. I'm actually good friends with Mandy, so I can see what she thinks and if they are able to handle a wedding your size."

"I hope they can. I'd really love to have their eggplant parm as one of our vegetarian options."

When they finished, Lisa spoke up. She'd mostly been listening and nodding as Angela had gone through what she wanted for her wedding.

"So, I just wanted to let you both know you are invited this Sunday to a sixtieth birthday party I'm having for Rhett. Philippe, too, of course. It's kind of a last-minute thing."

"Will it be a surprise?" Mia asked.

Lisa smiled and there was a gleam in her eye. "You could say that."

MIA TOOK HERSELF OUT TO LUNCH THE NEXT DAY. SHE had been craving the eggplant parmesan from Mimi's Place since Angela had mentioned it, and she wanted to say hello to Mandy anyway and chat with her about possibly catering Angela's wedding. They'd become good friends over the past six months as Mia had done several weddings that had either had the reception at Mimi's Place or had them cater it. The restaurant had changed hands a little over a year ago when the owner died and left it to her three granddaughters and the chef, equally. Mandy and her sister, Emma, ran the front of the restaurant while Paul, the chef, managed the kitchen. Their other sister, Jill, was a mostly silent partner and ran a recruiting business in Manhattan.

Mia stopped in at a quarter to two, as the lunch

service was winding down. She knew Mandy would have more time to chat during the slower time. Mandy's sister Emma was at the front desk and smiled when she saw her.

"Hi, Mia. Do you need a table for lunch?"

"I'm going to just grab a seat at the bar, I think. Is Mandy here today?"

"She is. She's in the kitchen talking to Paul. I'll let her know to stop by and say hello when she comes back out."

Mia settled at the bar, which was empty except for an older gentleman who was sipping coffee and nibbling on tiramisu while he fiddled with a crossword puzzle. The bar was small, with about a dozen seats. Mia liked eating at the bar, especially if she was by herself. She also liked chatting with Gina, one of the bartenders. Gina smiled when she saw her.

"Hey, Mia. Are you eating today?"

Mia nodded. "Yes, and I don't even need a menu. I'll have the eggplant parmesan, a salad with the house Italian dressing and a club soda with lemon."

"Perfect, I'll put that right in." Gina punched the order into the computer and returned a few minutes later with Mia's soda water, salad and a small basket of bread and butter. Mia tore off a chunk of bread and was spreading butter on it when Mandy came over and gave her a hug.

"Nice to see you. Are you meeting anyone today?"

Mia shook her head. "Nope, just me."

Mandy smiled and slid into the chair next to her. "Good, I can sit and visit with you for a while then. It's slow and Emma is on tonight, so I'm finishing early. What's new and exciting with you? We need a girls' night soon."

"We do. My schedule is way more open than yours, so let me know what works for you." Mandy was recently divorced and had two children, so nights out had to be scheduled and planned for in advance.

"Hm, possibly Friday night. Let me see if I can line up a sitter and I'll let you know."

They chatted for a bit, catching up on the situation with Mia's condo.

"Hopefully, it will be ready in a few weeks. It doesn't look like it's going to take as long as we originally thought."

"That's a relief. I'm sure you'll be happy to get back there and sleep in your own bed."

"Yes, though it's really not bad at all being at The Beach Plum Cove Inn. I almost feel like I'm on vacation. Penny and I have been walking the beach every day, and it includes a full breakfast. It's nice chatting with Kate's mom in the morning, too."

"I've met Lisa. She's very nice. She came to our big open house when we relaunched Mimi's Place."

"That was a fun night and a great idea you had to do that. Which reminds me, I met with a new client yesterday. Maybe you know them, Angela and her fiancé, Philippe Gaston?"

Mandy laughed. "Everyone on Nantucket knows Philippe. He and Angela were just in here last week for dinner, actually, and we were chatting."

"Well, they'd love to have you handle the catering for the wedding. But it's going to be huge, six hundred and fifty, maybe a few more even. I wasn't sure if that was something you'd want to take on?"

"Wow. Well, I'm thrilled she thought of us. My first instinct is to say yes…but I'm not the one that will be cooking all that food. Let me check with Paul and see what he thinks. What date did they have in mind?"

"She said ideally in two months or so. It sounds like they are flexible."

"Will it be a fancy plated dinner? What did she have in mind?"

"Something a little more casual, a beach buffet. Italian themed. She mentioned eggplant as one of the options."

Mandy nodded. "That's good. A beach buffet will be much more manageable for a party that size. I'll go check with Paul now. Stay tuned."

Mandy headed into the kitchen and a few minutes later Gina returned with Mia's eggplant parmesan. It was steaming hot, so Mia let it cool for a moment before digging in. She loved the way Mimi's Place made their eggplant. It was sliced really thin and lightly pan-fried with just a dusting of flour before it was layered like a lasagna with cheese and baked until bubbly. She'd just taken her first bite when Mandy returned with an excited look and slid into her chair.

"Paul says we can do it. He'll just staff extra people that day to make sure the restaurant is covered for their regular service. For the weddings, he does as much of the prep work as possible ahead of time. And of course, I'll be there to help coordinate it all, too."

"Perfect. It will be fun to do this wedding together. We make a good team."

"We really do," Mandy agreed. They'd done four weddings together so far over the past year and had two more booked in the next six months. Mia liked Mandy as a friend, but really liked working with her, too, because they had similar styles. Both were very organized and planned well, so no details were overlooked, and things generally went smoothly.

"Do you want to put a proposal together and I can go over it with Angela?" Mia suggested.

"I'll get something off to you tomorrow. We have some new menu additions that might be fun for her to consider."

"Oh, like what?" Mia never tired of discussing food.

"Well, we just did this at a recent wedding, and it was a huge hit. Paul made tiny cheeseburgers on those melt-in-your-mouth brioche buns. They're snack size and they bring them out along with fries towards the end of the night."

"Oh, that's a great idea!"

"It really is, especially if people have been drinking or didn't eat much earlier and danced up an appetite." A moment later she asked, "How's Izzy doing? I haven't seen her in a while."

"She's good. I'm not so sure about her boyfriend, though. I'm not a fan," Mia admitted.

"Oh, no. I thought you liked him?"

"I never spent much time around him until recently when I stayed there for a few days right after the fire." She told Mandy about Rick's moodiness and his temper.

"Hm. That doesn't sound promising. Your sister is too sweet to have to deal with that."

"I know. She says she loves him, though, and wants to try to make it work."

"That's a tough one, then. There's not much you can do, except be there for her."

"Right. I just worry about her."

Mandy smiled. "Of course, you do. Why don't you see if she can come out with us on Friday? I should be able to get a sitter. I'll let you know for sure tomorrow."

"That sounds good. I think she'd probably love to join us."

CHAPTER 11

Mia woke the next day feeling unusually blue for no apparent reason. It wasn't until she was sitting downstairs at breakfast enjoying her first cup of coffee with Lisa and Rhett that she realized what the date was, and her eyes immediately welled with tears. She tried to fight them back, to compose herself before Lisa noticed, but she wasn't fast enough.

"Mia, honey, what's wrong?"

Mia took a deep breath. "It's nothing. I'm fine. I just…well, I just realized what today's date is. It was Mark's birthday. I still get caught off-guard sometimes, especially on the holidays. I thought I was almost past this."

"Don't be so hard on yourself. Grief doesn't have a timetable. It's different for everyone. My first year was the hardest, like everyone says. But I still have occasional pangs of sadness on those dates—birthdays, anniversaries, when his favorite song comes on the radio. It all depends how you're feeling at that moment, too. Sometimes it just hits you harder."

Mia nodded. "Thanks. It helps to hear that."

Lisa was quiet for a moment. "Have you ever talked with anyone? A therapist or a bereavement group?"

"No. No one. Izzy suggested I talk to someone, but I never did. It's funny, Kate just mentioned a bereavement group the other day. A friend of hers told her about it. She gave me the information, but I haven't done anything about it yet."

"Maybe you should. I went to a group like that. None of my friends had gone through it and even though they meant well, they couldn't really understand. But everyone in the group knew what it was like. A few of them have become good friends. It helps to talk to people that have been through it."

"Maybe I'll check it out. Can't hurt, I suppose."

THE REST OF MIA'S DAY WAS BUSY, AND SHE DIDN'T GIVE the bereavement group another thought until late afternoon. It had been a long day. Bethany was turning out to be a potential Bridezilla, and Mia was exhausted by the time she finished with her and headed home. Bethany had agonized over every tiny decision and kept adding demands to her list of must-haves.

Mia thought she was kidding when she asked for a live zebra to roam the reception because she thought it would look really cool and she'd seen it on a reality show. Mia gently reminded her, because she'd seen the same episode, that the show was set in Hollywood and the likelihood of having zebras available in Massachusetts that could also travel to Nantucket was unlikely. Bethany pouted but agreed to settle for goat yoga at her brunch the day after her bachelorette party.

Mia was on her way home and was planning to just heat up some soup for dinner, take Penny for a walk and have an early night, when the song *Marry Me* by Train came on the car radio and she felt the sharpest pain she'd felt in a very long time. That had been the song they were going to dance to at their wedding. It made her heart ache listening to it, but she couldn't change the channel.

By the time she reached the inn, the song was long over, but her eyes were still damp, and she knew her nose was red. She parked the car, grabbed her cell phone and her purse, and a scrap of paper fell out of it. She picked it up and sighed. It was the address that Kate had given her for the bereavement group. It felt like a sign. It was Wednesday, and the group met Wednesday nights at six at Janie's Yoga Studio, which was just off Main Street. If Mia hurried, she would just about have time to walk Penny, have a little soup and head to the meeting.

AT A FEW MINUTES PAST FIVE THIRTY, MIA SET OUT TO GO to the bereavement group meeting. She wanted to get there early to introduce herself and make sure it was okay for her to join them. She really didn't know what to expect.

When she reached the yoga studio, there were a few cars in the parking lot and when she opened the door, she could see that the room was set up for a meeting. A circle of a dozen chairs was in the middle of the room, and on a side table there was a platter of cookies and brownies, and a thermos of coffee. A tall, slender woman with shoulder length, slightly graying brown hair stood chatting by the coffee table. She smiled when she saw Mia walk in and went to welcome her.

"Are you here for the bereavement group?" Her voice was warm and kind, and Mia relaxed a bit. She had tensed up when she first walked in.

"Yes, it's my first time."

"Well, welcome. I'm Janie Paul, the owner of the yoga studio. I'm also a retired social worker. I started this group when a friend's husband passed a few years back and have kept it going."

"I'm Mia Maxwell."

"I'm glad you joined us, Mia. There's coffee and some cookies and brownies if you'd like to grab a snack. We'll get started in a few more minutes."

"Thank you." Mia made her way to the side table and helped herself to a brownie. She nibbled it while she looked around the room. A few more people came in and stopped to chat with Janie. She noticed there was a mix of ages, from late twenties to seventies. She wondered if Kate's friend Sam was coming.

She finished her brownie just as Janie called for everyone to be seated.

"Grab a seat everyone, wherever you like."

Mia sat next to a woman who looked to be in her early fifties. She smiled and introduced herself. "I'm Barbara. Is this your first time here?"

Mia nodded. "Yes. I'm Mia."

"It's a good group, Mia. I hope you like it."

The only empty seat was next to Mia, but then the front door opened, and a man came rushing in and apologized quickly before taking it. "I'm so sorry. My babysitter was running late."

"It's fine, Sam. We haven't started yet." Janie looked around the circle before speaking again. "So, let's go around the group, introduce ourselves and share how we're feeling today. It's up to you how much or how little you share. Whatever you are comfortable with."

Mia felt herself tense up again. She had that feeling like when she was in school, didn't know the answer to the question and was hoping that she wouldn't get called on. Mia hoped Janie would start with someone else, so she could listen and get a feel for what she should say.

"Sam, why don't you start us off," Janie suggested.

The man next to her smiled and Mia realized unless there was another Sam in the room, that he was probably Kate's friend, the one that had suggested she come here. She was curious to hear what he had to say.

"Hi everyone, I'm Sam. I lost my wife Mary a little over a year ago to breast cancer. I have twin seven-year-old daughters, Becky and Sarah. I've been here on

Nantucket now for about a month. My parents are here and we live right down the street from them. Which has been great. My mother has been babysitting and the girls love seeing them. So, things are much better now than they were a month ago. But some days are still hard.

"Mary was my wife, but she was also my best friend, and I just really miss her. Some days more than others. Today was one of those days. I was driving along, and her favorite song came on the radio. She used to always sing along whenever we were in the car together, and it just hit me hard. But then I went home, and my girls ran over to see me, and it lifted my mood. So, overall, things are looking up. Just out of the blue, sometimes it still hits me hard."

Mia looked around the room and saw that most people were nodding. They all understood. Janie motioned for the older gentleman next to Sam to go next and Mia realized she'd be last, which she appreciated. It gave her a chance to listen to everyone's stories and to get to know them a bit.

"I'm Ken and it's been six months since my Susan passed. We were married for fifty years. Today was a good day. Susan never let me in the kitchen, she said that was her territory, and she was a darn good cook, so I didn't argue with her about it. But I didn't know how to even boil water. My granddaughter had to teach me how to cook, and I picked it up okay. I can make hotdogs and beans just fine. But a few days ago, she taught me how to bake a cake. And that was something else! You just open a box, dump it in a bowl with oil and eggs, and then bake it. So, when I went to the store today, I noticed there was a sale on those cake mix boxes and I bought a half dozen of 'em. Those brownies on the side table? I made those myself, just this afternoon! So, that's all I have to say."

"Ken, your brownies came out great," Barbara said. A few others chimed in and Ken looked pleased. They continued on around the group. Some people were in worse shape than others. The ones who had lost a loved one more recently were having the most difficult time. Candy, who was the youngest, had lost her husband only three months ago to a drunk driver.

"Yesterday would have been our one-year wedding anniversary. We were going to go to New York City for the weekend and see Hamilton on Broadway. I just can't believe he's gone. I don't feel like things are ever going to be normal again. Yesterday was just really tough. It hit me a lot harder than I realized it would."

"I'm sorry, Candy," Janie said. She looked around the group. "I know you've all heard that the first year is the hardest and that it will get better after that. But please know that everyone is different, and it's okay to feel what you're feeling."

Finally, it was Mia's turn.

"Hi, I'm Mia. I lost my fiancé a little over a year ago in a car accident. It happened two weeks before our wedding. I work as a wedding planner, too, and I love my job. But it was hard for a while, bittersweet. It has slowly been getting easier, like everyone said it would. But I think I expected it to just stop after a year and to feel normal again. And I'm still sad. Not as bad, but it's still there, and it hits me sometimes when I least expect it. A friend thought it might help for me to come here, but I wasn't sure about it. Earlier today, when I was on my way home, the song *Marry Me* came on the radio and that was going to be our first dance song. I lost it a little and thought maybe it wouldn't hurt to come tonight."

Janie smiled. "Well, we're very glad that you did." She looked around the room. "Does anyone else have any news they want to share?"

Barbara raised her hand. "I do. I just wanted to let you all know that this will be my last meeting. I'm moving off-island next week. It's all good, though. I've been coming here since Janie started the group almost three years ago, and I've stayed because many of you have become good friends. Some of you already know this, but I got engaged last week. I never thought I'd meet anyone, let alone get married again, but I met David while out walking Molly, my dog. We became friends and—well, fell in love. Neither one of us expected it. David was offered a wonderful teaching opportunity at a college in Boston, so we are moving to Somerville."

Mia was impressed. She knew from her introduction that Barbara had been married for almost thirty years and that her husband had died suddenly of a heart attack. If she could get through this and start over again with someone new, it gave Mia hope that she could get through it, too. She wasn't thinking about dating, though. It still felt too soon for that.

They spent the rest of the hour talking about what everyone had found worked best when they were having a bad day. By the time the meeting ended, Mia was glad that she went and felt hopeful that the weekly meetings would help.

When the meeting broke up, Sam turned to her. "You must be Kate's friend?"

"And you're Sam." Mia immediately felt a little flustered. "I mean, Kate mentioned that you found the group helpful. Thank you for giving her the information."

"Of course."

"Sam, we're heading to the Rose and Crown. Why don't you invite this pretty new lady to join us?" Ken said.

Sam smiled. "Thanks, Ken. I was just about to." He turned to Mia. "A bunch of us usually head out for a quick bite to eat after the meetings. Why don't you join us?"

Mia saw Ken and Barbara and a few others, even Candy, waiting by the door. It had been a good night, and she wasn't anxious to get home.

"Sure, I'd love to." Mia grabbed her coat and purse and they walked over to join the others. The Rose and Crown pub was just a few streets over, an easy five-minute walk from the yoga studio. It wasn't busy, and they were quickly led to a big round table. The Rose and Crown was a restaurant bar, with lots of dark wood and a casual menu. There were six of them—Sam, Mia, Barbara, Ken, Candy and Janie.

Everyone ordered a drink, except Janie, who had a hot tea. They ordered a few appetizers for the table—nachos, clam fritters and chicken wings. Sam and Ken both ordered burgers as well, and Janie got a bowl of chowder. They stayed for just about an hour, and Mia was surprised by the shift in mood. Everyone, except for Ken, had been so serious and sad at the meeting. But here, they were all joking and laughing, and it was a really fun time. She got a big kick out of Ken, who flirted shamelessly with the waitresses, but he was very sweet, and they seemed to adore him. When he spoke about his wife, which was often, it was clear that they'd been madly in love right up until the end.

Mia knew that Sam had grown up on Nantucket, too, and went to school with Kate.

"What's it like moving home? Are many of your friends still here?" she asked.

"It's great being back, to be near my family, and the girls love it. Besides Kate and one or two others, though, most of the people I knew in school moved off-island after college and we've lost touch. There aren't as many year-round opportunities here, and I think a lot of us wanted to stretch our wings and see what it was like to live where we don't have to depend on a ferry or plane to get somewhere."

"That did take some getting used to," Mia agreed. "I almost moved home about a year after living here, when my mother was sick, and I had to get back to the city fast. The weather was rough, and the boats weren't running, and I almost didn't get a flight, either. I made it on the last one out before they shut that down, too. But my mother was fine. And I realized if the boats stop running, I'd rather be here than there. This is home now for me.

Though my mother hasn't accepted that yet. She's still hopeful that I'll come to my senses and move back to Manhattan."

Sam laughed. "I don't think I could ever live in a big city like that."

"My parents love it. They don't understand how neither one of their children appreciates it. My sister Izzy lives here, too. Do you have any brothers or sisters?"

He shook his head. "No, it's just me, so my parents are pretty excited that I've moved back."

"Is it temporary? Or do you think you'll stay?"

"I'm planning to stay. It's a good place to raise kids, and it's hard to be a single parent. My mother has been a huge help."

"I bet she loves having you all here."

Sam smiled. "She does. It's been good for all of us."

Mia turned her attention to Barbara as Janie asked, "So, Barbara, tell us more about your fiancé."

"And how come you never mentioned him before?" Ken added.

Barbara smiled. "I never mentioned him because I was afraid it was too good to be true and that I might jinx it. After I met him walking my dog, we ran into each other a few more times and then he suggested lunch and I liked that. It didn't seem as serious as dinner. I told him if he'd suggested dinner, I might have said no!"

Mia smiled as she looked around the table. She liked these people, liked that they were all happy for each other and that they were going through similar struggles. When everyone was finished, they got the check and split it evenly. Ken made them laugh as they walked back to the yoga studio.

"That waitress told me to friend her on Facebook. I have no idea what that means."

"How old is your granddaughter that taught you to cook?" Mia asked.

"She's about your age—early thirties, right?"

Mia nodded. "Right. Why don't you ask her to show you how Facebook works? It's a great way to keep in touch with people and you can see pictures that your friends and family members are posting."

"And if she gets me on the Facebook, I can be that waitress's friend?"

Mia laughed. "Yes, you can send her a friend request."

"Okay, got it. Friend request."

Everyone said their goodbyes when they reached the parking lot.

"It was nice meeting you, Mia. Will we see you again next week?" Sam asked.

Mia didn't hesitate. "Yes, I'll be back."

CHAPTER 12

"So, how was the bereavement group?" Izzy asked. It was Friday night and Mia, Mandy and Izzy were sipping chardonnay in the bar of the Club Car restaurant, which was right on Main Street. The food was good, and it was always a crowded after-work spot, especially on a Friday night. They'd just shared a few appetizers and were relaxing and people-watching.

"It was better than I expected, actually."

"Oh, good. Does that mean you'll be going back?" Izzy asked.

"I will. They're a nice bunch of people. It was helpful to talk to them. You were right."

Izzy smiled. "I'm glad to hear it."

"What is Rick up to tonight?" Mandy asked.

"He's out with a few friends."

"How are things going with him? Any leads on a new job?" Mia worried that no one would hire him after he'd been fired from his last two companies.

"He started yesterday, actually. Another friend hooked him up. So, they'll be working together, and they get along well, so fingers crossed that third time's the charm. He is really good at what he does."

"That's great news. Tell him I said congratulations," Mia said.

Izzy smiled. "I will. Thanks." She turned to Mandy. "How's everything with your new man?"

Mandy blushed. "Fine. We're taking things slow. We're getting to know each other. He seems like a really nice guy." Mandy was recently divorced after learning her husband was cheating. She wasn't looking at all, but she had met a really nice guy that ran a boat business on Nantucket, like her grandfather did years ago. They hit it off right away.

"I told him no, the first time he asked me out," Mandy said. "Fortunately for me, he didn't give up."

"Isn't that your neighbor, Ben?" Izzy was looking at the far end of the bar where three tall guys wearing golf shirts and shorts were laughing and drinking draft beers. One of them was Ben.

"That's him." A moment later, three women joined them, all young, and with perfect figures. Mia recognized one of them as the woman who'd been stumbling in the hallway on Mia's first night at the inn.

"Is that his girlfriend?" Izzy asked.

"I don't know. I've only seen her at the inn once before. Could be."

Ben looked around the room and smiled when he saw Mia. A minute later, he was heading their way.

"Happy Friday, ladies."

"Hi, Ben. You know Izzy, and this is my friend Mandy."

"Nice to meet you."

"Is that your girlfriend? I recognize her from when she was visiting."

Ben grinned. "The night we stumbled home, you mean? We used to date, but we're mostly just friends now."

Mia raised her eyebrows at that, and Ben tried to convince her.

"Really. She just crashed with me that night because neither one of us should have been driving. I took her home as soon as we got up the next day."

Mia laughed and changed the subject. "Are you all having dinner here? We just had some appetizers, and they were great."

Ben shook his head. "No, we already had a bite to eat at the club after our round of golf. We're just here for a few drinks. I should probably get back over to them. Just wanted to say hello. Maybe I'll see you at breakfast tomorrow."

Mia smiled. "You think you'll be up that early?"

He laughed. "You're right, it's doubtful. See you all later."

They watched him head back to his friends and as soon as he reached them, the girl Mia recognized pulled Ben over and put her arm around his shoulders.

"They look like more than friends to me," Izzy said.

"He's very handsome. And rich. He's your neighbor?" Mandy asked.

Mia nodded. "Present and future. He's at the inn, and he's the owner of the unit next to mine."

"Interesting. He seems nice enough and possibly single. He might be fun for you to date."

Mia laughed. "Assuming we're both interested in that. I'm not, and I doubt he is, either."

"He'd really be perfect though. You're not looking for anything serious, probably not for a long time. He doesn't strike me as the serious type, and I bet he'd be a lot of fun to do things with. Just keep it in mind. Maybe he could teach you to golf!"

Mia laughed again. "You're crazy."

"Have you ever been to that golf course? It's gorgeous. Cory has a membership there. I used to like to go. Part of my divorce settlement is that I still have a membership. I'm a terrible golfer, but it's fun to try anyway and they have a nice restaurant and bar. We should go sometime."

Mia had never been to the Nantucket Golf Club. It was relatively new, and very expensive. She remembered reading somewhere that the initiation fee to join was half a million dollars. That was a drop in the bucket for Mandy's ex-husband, though. Cory Lawson ran a very successful hedge fund and made many millions every year.

Places like that reminded her of the world she'd grown up in. Her parents belonged to a similar club in the Hamptons, and when she was younger, it had been fun to go to all the different events. But she preferred her more modest life on Nantucket. There were plenty of crazy rich people here, mostly in the summer, but Mia preferred the more laid-back, year-round crowd. She did really like Mandy, though, so if Mandy invited Mia to that fancy club, it probably would be a fun time.

An hour or so later, when Mandy fought back a yawn and realized she had to get back for the sitter, they asked for their check. As they were leaving, Mia turned at the sound of loud laughter and saw that it was coming from Ben's group. Ben was animated as he was telling a story and his friends were enjoying it immensely. Mandy smiled.

"See, I told you he looks fun."

AS PREDICTED, BEN DIDN'T MAKE IT DOWN TO BREAKFAST. Mia slept in, too, and went down later than she normally did and missed eating with Lisa and the girls. She knew she'd be seeing them the next day, though, for Rhett's birthday party. She had the room to herself and read the news on her phone while she drank her coffee and ate a banana nut muffin.

On her way back to her room, she ran into Ben who was just coming down the stairs. He stopped when he saw her.

"What are you doing right now?"

"I was just heading back to my room and thinking about doing laundry. Why?"

"Want to take a ride with me? I'm heading over to the condos to meet Will. We can see how things are progressing. Aren't you curious?"

"I am, actually. Sure, I'll go with you." She followed him to his car, a red Jeep Wrangler, and hopped in the passenger side.

Ben seemed full of energy. Mia guessed it hadn't been a late night. She never heard him come in, though. She fell asleep as soon as her head hit the pillow.

"Did you guys have fun last night?" she asked.

"It was a good time. We left about a half hour after you did. We had an early start, after golfing. Do you golf?"

"I never have. Someday I'll try it."

"You really should. It's a great game. We could go hit some balls sometime if you want? I can show you how to swing. That's the most important thing. If you get that right, you're good."

The offer took her by surprise. "That sounds fun. I don't have any equipment, though."

"Okay, we'll figure it out. I can borrow a few of Bethany's clubs. You guys are about the same height. And her clubs are just collecting dust in the garage."

Mia was pretty sure that golf was the last thing on Bethany's mind.

A few minutes later, they reached the condos. Will was hard at work in Ben's unit, along with two helpers. They had just finished laying the new flooring, which looked gorgeous. Ben had gone with a more common, lighter shade and the sun coming through the windows and the pretty wood floor made the room glow.

"Oh, that looks gorgeous," Mia said.

"It does look pretty good," Ben agreed.

"Thanks. It's not done yet," Will said. "But it's getting there. Hold on a sec, and I'll get those samples." He went into another room then returned with three polished wood samples for Ben to choose from for his office furniture. They were all lovely. Ben chose the color that was in the middle, a rich brown but not too dark or light.

"So, timing-wise, I'd say two more weeks. You should be able to move in the weekend after Memorial Day."

"That's fantastic," Ben said.

"Mia, do you want to take a peek at your place? Your floors are down, too, and they look beautiful. I still need to seal them, though."

Mia and Ben followed Will next door to Mia's unit. He opened the door, and when they all stepped inside, Mia's jaw dropped. Her eyes started to water, too, and she blinked quickly to chase the tears away. But they were happy tears. The hardwood floors looked gorgeous, so much prettier than the old carpeting. She could already picture her furniture and the new throw rugs she was going to buy.

"They look wonderful, Will. Thank you."

"It did turn out pretty nice, if I do say so." Will was proud of his work, as he should be.

"So, plan on two weeks. I'll text you a few days before I'm completely done."

They said goodbye to Will and hopped back in the

Jeep. Ben started to head back toward the inn, but as they approached the road to his mother's house he turned to Mia. "You said you have nothing important going on, right? Just laundry?"

Mia nodded. "Right."

"Well, let's go have that golf lesson now. We can swing by the house and grab the clubs. Mine are in the back of the jeep. We can go to the driving range and hit some balls. The weather couldn't be more perfect for it. We should be outside, not home doing laundry." He made a face and Mia laughed.

"Sure. Let's do it."

The only one home was Bethany. She was sitting in the sunroom, surrounded by wedding invitations and envelopes that needed addressing. She looked up in surprise when she saw the two of them walk in together.

"Can we borrow a few of your golf clubs?" Ben asked her.

Bethany laughed. "Sure, take them all if you want. I won't be using them anytime soon." She looked at Mia. "Do you golf?"

"Not yet. Your brother offered to show me how to hit."

"We're going to the driving range. We're neighbors now, you know. Neighbors do things like that." He turned to go, and Bethany looked at Mia curiously. "My brother is a nut. Have fun, you two."

Ten minutes later, they reached the driving range. It wasn't too crowded as Ben explained the weather was so good that most people were actually out golfing, not just hitting balls. He put her clubs in his bag and carried them to an open hitting tee.

Mia watched as Ben carefully explained what he was doing and why. He demonstrated a few swings. Then handed her a club.

"Okay, it's your turn now. Remember what I said, keep your arms straight and your eyes on the ball."

Mia tried to focus and do what Ben had told her. She kept her arms straight, brought the club back, swung hard and missed.

"Don't worry about it. Try again. Stay down. You came up on your toes."

She did, taking a deep breath and staying down. She hit the ball, but it didn't go where she thought she'd aimed. Instead, it veered sharply to the left.

"That's great!" Ben looked thrilled, but she shook her head.

"That was not good."

"You hit the ball! That's the first step. Keep going."

And she did. Mia hit ball after ball after ball. And after a while, they started going where she wanted them to. She hit one that made a really cool sound, a loud crack followed by a whoosh, and the ball sailed up and out and straight. It was her best shot by far, and it felt different from the others.

Ben gave her a high five. "Now that was a golf shot. See if you can do it again."

But her next shot was horrible. It went to the left again and she couldn't understand it. She thought she'd done everything exactly the same.

Ben grinned. "Welcome to the mystifying, frustrating world of golf. It's a mental game as much as a physical one. But the more you practice, the easier it gets. You tired yet? Or do you want to hit a few more?"

"I'll hit a few more. It's kind of addicting. I want another good shot."

"All right, then. You can do it."

And she did. Mia's next three shots were her best yet. They hit for another twenty minutes and then they were both ready to go.

"Are you getting hungry?" Ben asked as they drove off. "We could grab some sandwiches from Claudette's and bring them back to the inn. Have you ever had the meatloaf sandwich from there?"

Mia laughed. "I've never had a meatloaf sandwich period."

"You haven't lived then until you've had one—and Claudette's is the best. You can get normal stuff, too, turkey or roast beef."

"Well, now you have me curious. I'll try a meatloaf sandwich."

Ben drove to Claudette's Sandwich Shop, ordered the sandwiches and when they were ready, Mia held the bag while they drove home.

When they reached the inn, they decided to eat outside, since it was still so nice out. Lisa had pointed out a common area in the back yard that was available for any of the guests to use. There were two outside wooden tables, chairs and a small grill. They brought their sand-wiches to one of the tables. Once they were settled, Mia unwrapped her sandwich and took a bite. A cold meatloaf sandwich had sounded a little strange, but Ben was right. It was delicious.

"So, Mia, tell me more about yourself. What do you like to do for fun? Are you dating anyone?"

"There's not a lot to tell. I mostly work and see friends. I'm not dating anyone. I'm not sure when I'll be ready for that."

Ben nodded. "It must be hard. How long has it been?"

"Just over a year."

"It has been a year, though? So, you should be ready to date soon?"

Mia laughed. "It's like something magical is supposed to happen at the one-year mark, like a switch is flipped and everything goes back to normal. I wish that was the case. I'm getting there. But I still can't think of anyone but Mark. I'm sure that will change one day."

"Yeah, I'm sure."

"So, what about you? Are you dating anyone? You're sure that girl I saw you with is just a friend?"

"Oh, I'm very sure. I date whenever the opportunity presents itself. There's no one serious, though. I haven't met that special someone yet. When I do, I might be ready to settle down."

"Do you really think so?" Mia couldn't picture it.

"Maybe. I'd like to think so. Meanwhile, life is pretty good."

Mia smiled. Life was very good indeed for Ben Billings.

They finished eating and Mia surprised herself by eating every last crumb of her sandwich. She gathered up her trash and stood to go. "Thank you for the golf lesson and for lunch. I'm off to tackle that laundry. What are you up to for the rest of the day?"

Ben yawned. "I think a nap might be in order. Then I'm playing golf later this afternoon."

They walked inside and went upstairs to their rooms. Ben paused as Mia unlocked her door. "Next step is to get you out on the golf course."

Mia froze. She didn't feel anywhere ready for that yet. "Shouldn't I hit balls again first?"

"Sure, but next time we'll hit balls then go play nine holes. Maybe one day next week your boss will let you duck out early and we can go?"

Mia grinned. "I'll see if I can talk my boss into it."

"Good. That was fun, Mia. You did great." He turned to unlock his door, and she did the same. It had been a fun day. Maybe Mandy was right about Ben.

CHAPTER 13

"Do you really think he'll like it? It's hard to know what to get someone who has everything." Kate held up the navy button-down dress shirt that she'd bought for Rhett for his birthday.

"I like it. So, he'll probably like it. And if he doesn't, he'll say he does and love that you got him something." Jack wrapped his arms around her and kissed her before saying, "So stop worrying."

"Okay. Hand me the scissors, would you? They're next to you, on the table." Jack did as requested, and Kate quickly wrapped the gift. They were due at her mother's by noon and, as usual, Kate was running late and rushing.

As soon as possible, they were on their way and were just two minutes late, which to Kate was as good as early. They were the last to arrive, though. The whole family was there, as well as her mother's best friends, Sue and her husband Curt, and Paige and her boyfriend Peter.

Angela and Philippe, Rhett's daughter, Michelle, and Mia rounded out the guest list.

Kate noticed that there were rows of seats in the backyard which she thought was a little strange for a birthday party. Her mother's eyes lit up when she saw Kate and Jack.

"Rhett, Kate's here. We can start now."

Kate thought her mother was acting strangely. She didn't usually fuss so much over birthdays. Rhett was by her side, beaming. Kate was surprised when he stepped forward and spoke.

"I'd like to thank you all for coming. Could you please go outside to where the chairs are set up? Your mother gave me the best birthday present ever by agreeing to marry me—today." He paused to let that sink in.

"Mom, are you…" Kristen began.

"Yes, we are! So, head outside everyone. Chase, I could use your help, please."

Kate and Jack followed the others outside and took a seat. Kate noticed a woman minister she'd never seen before standing next to Rhett and it suddenly seemed very real. Her mother was about to get married.

Rhett bent over and clicked something on a CD player, and suddenly the traditional wedding music began to play. All heads turned to watch Lisa, escorted by Chase, walk down the makeshift aisle to where Rhett and the minster were waiting. Chase took his seat and the minister began to speak.

"Lisa and Rhett would like to thank you all for joining them on this special day." She began the simple wedding service and when she got to the vows, said, "Lisa and Rhett have written their own vows. Rhett, what would you like to say to Lisa?"

Rhett took Lisa's hand and looked deep into her eyes as he spoke from his heart.

"Lisa, I came to the inn for a few weeks, but once I met you, got to know you and to love you, I knew I was home. I don't ever want to leave you. I will love you always."

"And Lisa, what would you like to say to Rhett?"

"Rhett, you were my first guest. Opening the inn allowed me to stay on Nantucket. I never expected to find love again. And then you walked in. I'm so grateful to have you in my life. I love you so much."

They exchanged rings and then the minister announced, "Lisa, Rhett, I now pronounce you husband and wife. Rhett, you may kiss your bride!"

They all clapped and cheered as Rhett kissed Lisa, and then the two of them faced their guests. "And now it's time to celebrate!" Rhett kissed Lisa again and everyone gathered around them, hugging and offering congratulations.

"I can't believe you didn't tell us!" Kate said when she reached her mother.

Lisa smiled. "You have enough to worry about with planning your own wedding. We thought this would be easy and fun! And it was. None of you suspected a thing!" She looked very pleased with herself.

"Well, it would have been nice to get you a wedding gift. All I brought is a shirt for Rhett."

Lisa laughed. "I'm sure he'll love it. He could use a new shirt. Now let's go inside and eat. It's a lobster lover's brunch."

Kate's mother loved lobster. "That sounds good. What are we having?"

"The lobster quiche, of course, lobster chowder, and my new favorite appetizer, bite-sized pieces of lobster tail served with hot butter to dip them in."

"Yum!"

"How are you feeling about your wedding? Are you still stressed out?" Lisa asked.

"How did you know I was stressing about the wedding planning?" Kate thought she'd done a good job of not letting people know.

"I'm your mother. That's how I knew. Let Mia worry about everything. That's what she's there for, and she's very good at what she does."

"Thank you! And congratulations, Lisa!" Mia walked up in time to hear Lisa's comments.

"I'm really not that stressed," Kate told her.

Mia smiled. "It's okay. We're almost through the worst of it, and then you'll be able to relax. Once you pick out your dress, it's all downhill from there. And just let me know what's good for you this week and we'll zip into Boston for the day."

"I did like a few of those links that you sent me. I'm sorry I haven't gotten back to you. I've just been deep in my book."

"I figured as much. I wasn't going to bug you for a few more days," Mia said.

"Okay, well I could do this Tuesday if that works for you?"

"It does."

Lisa put a hand on each of their backs and led them into the house. "Now that we've got that sorted, let's go eat."

Kate went over to her mother's best friends to say hello. Both Sue and Paige had suspiciously shiny eyes. "I'm just so happy for your mother," Sue said.

"They're just so good together," Paige added.

"They really are," Kate agreed. She wondered if Paige might get engaged soon, too. She'd been dating Peter, the owner of Bradford's Liquors, for a while now and they seemed very happy, too.

Kate and Jack got plates of food and sat outside with Kristen and Tyler.

"I can't believe Mom pulled this off without anyone knowing what she was up to," Kristen said.

"I know. She really didn't want anything to do with a big wedding. This was exactly what she said she wanted, small and just close friends and family."

"You could still do something small like this, too, if you'd rather," Kristen said.

"It's tempting, but I think what we're planning will be fine. It won't be too big. All of mom's friends and Jack's father's friends and our families can all be there. And Mia really is a godsend. She's doing most of the work."

"Where is Mia?" Kristen asked.

Kate spotted her holding a plate of food and looking

around for a place to sit. She waved her over to join them.

"I have to say, I'm impressed. Your mother did a great job setting this up. None of you had any idea?" Mia asked.

Kate laughed. "Not a clue."

Lisa made the rounds, visiting with everyone, and told them about their honeymoon plans. They were leaving the next day, going to New York City for a few days, and were going to stop by Rhett's other restaurants as Lisa had never seen them.

"We'll be home on Friday in time for the craziness of Memorial Day weekend."

"Oh, good, then you're both coming to my cookout?" Kate said.

"Of course, honey. I wouldn't miss it."

Beth brought her plate over and joined them. Kate hadn't talked to her soon-to-be sister-in-law since the appetizer party. "How's the wedding planning coming for you?" Kate asked her. Beth and Chase worked together. Beth ran the office for Chase's construction business. She didn't have a lot of free time. Kate didn't know how she did it.

"It's going pretty well. All the major things have been decided and booked. Well, except the dress. I still need a dress. I've looked everywhere on the island, but nothing is right."

"Mia and I are going to Boston on Tuesday to look at dresses. You're welcome to join us."

"Hm. That is tempting. Let me check and see if I can do it. I might be able to move some things around."

"What have you decided on for a reception?"

"I think we're going to have it at Mimi's Place. I've been talking to Mandy there and they have some good packages."

"Oh, nice. Angela is using them, too. They are going to cater a beach buffet for over six hundred people."

Beth's eyes grew wide. "I can't even imagine. We're at about a hundred and fifty and it feels like a lot."

"That's Philippe. He does everything big, right, Angela?" Angela had just joined them.

"I was just telling Beth the size of your wedding. She's going to have Mimi's Place do her food, too."

"Oh, good! Yeah, I had to put my foot down when the number hit six hundred and fifty. Philippe was still adding people on a daily basis. We had to go back through the whole list and cross a few off so we'd have room for a few last-minute additions. Oh, by the way, the JCrew dress came, and it fits like a dream. Very happy to cross that off my list."

That reminded Kate to mention that Beth might join them for dress shopping on Tuesday.

"I hope you don't mind?"

Mia smiled. "No, the more the merrier. It will be a fun day."

CHAPTER 14

A little after ten on Tuesday morning, Mia picked up Kate and then Beth and drove to the Nantucket airport for their flight to Boston. If they'd taken the ferry, it would have eaten up too much of the day, as it was an hour on the fast ferry, then they'd have to rent a car and drive an hour and a half to Boston and deal with parking. Or if they took Mia's car, they'd have to take the slow boat which added another two hours of travel time to the day. So, they opted to fly instead and were in Boston less than an hour later. They took an Uber to Newbury Street, where they could walk to several bridal shops in the Back Bay area.

Newbury Street was where most of the expensive shopping was, and two of the bridal shops they were going to were about a block apart. The first shop was lovely, and they spent about an hour there, but none of the dresses felt like 'the one' to either Kate or Beth. They did a little better at the next shop. Kate still didn't have any luck, but Beth found her dream dress. It was the first one she tried on and it gave Mia goosebumps, it just looked so right on her. Kate felt it, too. Mia could tell by the look on her face when Beth walked out of the dressing room and swirled round in front of them.

"Do you like it? It feels nice on."

"Have you looked in the mirror yet? Turn around," Mia ordered.

Beth did and took a step back. "Wow."

"It looks beautiful on you," Mia said.

"I love it. I think I found my dress."

"I think you did, too. Hopefully, I'll have some luck, too," Kate said.

But none of the dresses she tried on there quite worked, and Mia could tell that Kate was getting discouraged.

"Why don't we have some lunch and relax a little before going to the third shop. I have a good feeling about that one. There were two dresses we really liked online."

"That sounds good. I am ready for a break, and I'm starving," Kate said.

They walked over to Boylston Street and to one of Mia's favorite Boston restaurants, Abe and Louie's. It was mostly a steakhouse, but they had wonderful salads, too, and good, crusty bread.

It was already almost one thirty, so the lunch rush was dying down and they were shown to a big booth with dark polished wood.

"Are you getting a drink? I think I might want something fun. They have some unusual cocktails here. There was one I really liked. Here it is, the gin and tonic with fresh strawberries and crushed black pepper. I want that."

"I think I'll have a mimosa," Mia said.

"Make that two," Beth told the waiter who appeared as they were discussing the drinks. When he returned, they all ordered the same thing—the signature salad with delicate Bibb lettuce, cinnamon dusted apple slices, pistachios, blue cheese and a Dijon vinaigrette. They added sliced filet mignon on top and finished the meal by splitting a crème brûlée.

They were all happily full and rested when they finished and headed to their last stop. Mia was feeling a little anxious, hoping that Kate would find something that worked here. There was another shop they could go to if they had to, in Beacon Hill, which wasn't too far, but it would add another hour at least to their stay in the city.

Kate was optimistic when they entered the third shop. It was full of beautiful dresses and an assistant brought them three glasses of champagne to sip while Kate tried on dress after dress. The two she had seen online were nice and looked lovely, but Mia agreed neither was quite right. Nor were the dozen other dresses. Kate was trying to keep her spirits up, but Mia could tell she was getting discouraged.

"Don't worry. I have a good feeling about the Beacon Hill shop. They are a little more expensive, but people rave about their dresses."

It was a warm day, so they decided to walk to Beacon Hill as it was a pretty walk through the public gardens and then Boston Common to Beacon Hill. They walked down Charles Street, the main street of Beacon Hill, until they reached Ceremony, which was on the third floor in a gorgeous loft. The shop had a magical feel to it as it was an eclectic curated collection of couture and independent designers. Mia relaxed a little when she saw Kate's face. She looked like a kid in a candy store.

"These are all so beautiful, and so *me*, I think." She picked three dresses to start with and the first two were beautiful, but when she walked out in the third dress, Mia got goosebumps again. It was so Kate. It was sleek and simple and shimmery and lacy, sleeveless with a dip in the back and fitted down to her knees where it then flared out a bit. It had a 1920s flapper look, but in a modern, sophisticated way. And Kate loved it.

"Finally. This is the one, I think."

"I think so, too," Mia agreed.

"Kate, you look absolutely beautiful."

Kate ordered the dress, and they told her it should arrive in about four months, which was perfect. She was thinking about the weekend of Christmas Stroll in December as a possible date. Beth was looking at Columbus Day Weekend in mid-October. Mia was glad that Angela had managed to find an off-the rack dress that fit, so there was no waiting time for it to be made to order. Her wedding was coming up quickly as they'd confirmed a date with Mandy for Mimi's Place to cater, the third Saturday in August.

And Bethany's wedding was the week before that. Mia was going to have a very busy August.

CHAPTER 15

When Wednesday night rolled around, Mia found herself looking forward to going to the six o'clock meeting at Janie's Yoga Studio. She was feeling strong overall and hadn't had any really sad moments in the past week, which was a first. She hoped it was a sign that things would continue to get easier. That the moments of sadness would come less often.

Ken was there when she arrived and was putting out a plate of small, bite-sized squares of white frosted cake.

"Did you make those?" Mia asked him.

"I did. It's spice cake with cream cheese frosting out of a can. Betty Crocker and me. Try a piece."

Mia popped a square in her mouth. It was delicious. Ken was right. Box cake mixes were the best. It was hard to screw them up. She gave him a thumbs-up.

"It's great. Thank you."

"Have another. I did cut them kind of small."

Sam came in a few minutes later and came over to say hello. He grabbed a paper plate and took two squares of cake and a chocolate chip cookie from the plate that Janie set out.

"I fed the kids dinner, but knew we were probably going out so didn't eat anything. Are you both coming out after the meeting?"

"Wouldn't miss it," Ken said.

"Me, too," Mia added.

Janie called everyone together, and the meeting got underway. Overall, it was a more upbeat night. Candy was still struggling, which was to be expected. But Ken, Sam and Mia all reported having good weeks.

The same group, minus Barbara, headed to the Rose and Crown when the meeting ended. They ordered the same appetizers as the week before and this time, Mia got a burger, too.

"How are the girls?" Mia asked Sam.

"They're good. They're looking forward to Kate's cookout next weekend. I think because I mentioned there might be s'mores. It's not like they know anyone there, except me."

Mia smiled. "Maybe they're just excited to get out and about."

"That's probably true. I'm going to take them down to the pier on Monday to watch all the boats leave. I think that's the best time to see them all. We might go on Saturday for a while, too, to see some of them sail in. The girls have never seen many big sailboats like that, and I think I got them curious. Plus, it's something to do."

"They will love it, I bet. The energy down at the pier is exciting on Figawi weekend. So many boats. Over two hundred, I think."

"When I was younger, I raced in it a few times. One of my friend's father had a nice sailboat and took us with him. It's quite a ride. These are serious sailors."

"That sounds fun. I've actually never been on a boat, other than the ferry."

"Being on a boat, a real sailboat is a blast. If you ever get the chance, you should go."

"Yeah, I will, definitely. I don't know anyone with a boat, but maybe one day."

Mia could picture the girls watching the boats with their dad and it occurred to her that she hadn't asked him how they were doing.

"How are the girls doing with their mom being gone? I meant to ask that earlier."

"It was really hard for them for the first few months. They both had trouble sleeping and Sarah went through a bed-wetting period. But they seem pretty good now. They rebounded faster than their dad did."

They were all quiet for a moment and then Ken spoke up. "It seems weird without Barbara here. She was always here, from the first week that I came."

"I miss her, too," Janie said. "Barbara was here when I first started the group. She could have stopped coming a long time ago, but once she felt stronger, she liked helping others get there, too. She was a good friend."

"Let's raise a glass to Barbara." Ken lifted his Kahlua

Sombrero, and they all lifted their glasses and in Janie's case, a teacup.

"To Barbara," Janie said.

"As much as I'm going to miss her, I think it should be encouraging for all of us that Barbara was able to move on, and to find love again. I know for a lot of us, it was hard to imagine that could happen," Janie said.

Ken nodded. "She was a nice lady, I'm happy for her. I don't see myself ever getting married again, but when I'm a little less sad, I won't rule out taking someone to dinner." He grinned. "I might have my pick to choose from. Ever since Susan died, there have been a few women that keep coming by to check on me. They bring me casseroles and cookies. Nice ladies. I get the feeling some of them might say yes if I asked."

"Ken, if you feel like going out to dinner with any of those ladies, you shouldn't hesitate. If you're not ready to call it romance, go out as friends. You might both enjoy the companionship. Then if it turns into something more, so be it," Janie advised.

"That's an interesting idea. I do like to go out to eat and I get tired of doing it by myself. If I make it clear that it's just as friends, you think they might be interested still?"

Janie smiled. "Why don't you ask and find out?"

"I'll do that." Ken turned to Sam and Mia. "What about you two? You both say you're not ready to get out there, but maybe you can make new friends, too, and see where that goes?"

Mia nodded, thinking of her day with Ben. Even

though there was nothing romantic there, it was still nice to get out and have fun.

"You might be onto something. I think I do need to get out more, too, and make some new friends. I can do that."

Sam grinned. "I think I could probably handle that, too. No pressure, just getting out more."

Candy took a sip of her wine and looked around the table. "I am most definitely not ready for any of that yet. But I'm glad you all are thinking about it, and it gives me something to look forward to. I hope I'm going to feel more like doing things soon."

"You will," Janie assured her. "Just give it time. All the time you need."

They enjoyed the rest of their evening, laughing over dinner at some of Ken's funny stories. He was retired, but had worked for years managing The Whitley, where Bethany wanted to have her reception. It was one of Nantucket's most exclusive hotels and had all kinds of interesting guests, many of them celebrities, and Ken shared that not all of them were well behaved. He didn't name any names, even though he no longer worked there.

"I bet that was a fun job. I'm actually planning a wedding that will be held there in August," Mia said.

"I loved working there, even when some guests drove us crazy. It's a special place and I'm sure they will do a wonderful job for her wedding." He smiled. "She'll pay dearly for it."

Mia laughed. "Yes, she will. But that's not a concern for her family."

"I heard a rumor that something is going on with the hotel, new management or something," Ken said. "It's been a while since I've talked to anyone from there. Have you heard anything?"

"No, I haven't heard a thing. I spoke to Sophie in sales a week or so ago to confirm the date for the wedding, and she didn't mention any changes."

"Maybe there was nothing to it, then. It was probably just a rumor."

When they finished eating, they walked back to their cars and said their goodbyes.

"See you at Kate's on Sunday?" Sam asked.

"Yes. I'm looking forward to it and to meeting your girls."

CHAPTER 16

"I'm having second thoughts about my dress," Bethany said. Mia was sitting in the sunroom with her and they were going over the menu options for the wedding and Bethany needed to choose what she wanted to try at the tasting the following week.

"What are you thinking about your dress?" Bethany was wearing her mother's dress that had been altered to fit her. There was no time to order a wedding dress at this point.

"I'm just not sure about it. Maybe I want something new?"

"I think the dress is lovely on you." Bethany had modeled it for Mia the last time she visited. "But if you do want to consider other options, it will have to be something off-the-rack."

Bethany pouted. "Are you sure? How long does it take to make a dress?"

"Four to five months, usually, sometimes longer."

"Oh. Well, maybe my mother's isn't so bad after all." She turned her attention back to the extensive menu options and picked several items in each category for the tasting.

"Great, I'll call them tomorrow or later today to let them know. How many people should I tell them to expect for the tasting?"

"Four. Me and Ryan, my mother and Ryan's mother."

Mia smiled. "Tastings are a lot of fun. It should be a lovely night."

"I think my mother and his mother are more excited about it than we are."

"Do you have any fun plans for the long weekend?" Mia asked.

"We do. Some of Ryan's friends are sailing in the Figawi, so we're going to have a house full of people. Ben is sailing in it, too. Has he mentioned it?"

"No. I haven't seen him all week. I didn't know he had a boat."

"He doesn't. But one of his good friends does. He stopped by this morning and said he's heading to Hyannis tonight for the pre-event festivities and is racing with them on Saturday." She looked at Mia curiously. "Doesn't he live right next door to you? You really haven't seen him at all?"

Mia laughed. "We have somewhat opposite schedules. I'm up and out early. I've only seen him at breakfast once since I moved in there. I'm usually in bed by the time he comes home at night."

Bethany nodded. "He always stayed out late. Did you guys have fun golfing the other day?"

"We did have fun. We didn't play golf, though. We just went to the driving range and Ben taught me how to swing. I'm a total beginner."

"He's a good teacher. You should get him to take you out on the golf course, too."

"He did mention possibly going soon. It feels like an imposition, though."

"Don't be silly. He wouldn't have offered if he wasn't willing."

"Okay. If he mentions it again, I'll take him up on it." Mia was glad that Bethany seemed to be in a good mood and much more laid back than the last time she'd seen her. Pretty much everything was done now. All Bethany had left to do was to go to her tasting next week and decide on her final menu. And there were no bad choices. Everything at The Whitley was exquisite. Mia thought about what Ken had mentioned, the rumor about a possible change in management. When she called Sophie with the details for the tasting, she'd ask her about that.

When Mia got back to the inn, she opened up her laptop, pulled up her notes on Bethany's choices and called them in to Sophie, her sales contact at The Whitley. Mia was about to hang up when she remembered to ask Sophie if there were any big management changes recently at The Whitley. "I heard a rumor and was just curious."

There was a long hesitation. "I really can't say anything about that, other than that The Whitley remains owned and managed by the Chapman family."

"Oh. Okay, thanks."

"It's my pleasure. Enjoy your weekend, Mia!" Mia smiled as she hung up the phone. Sophie's tone had changed so quickly from guarded to perky. She would have to let Ken know that there probably was something to the rumor, but they weren't saying anything just yet.

"Okay, Penny, let's go outside!" Mia took her for a walk on the beach, then came home and jumped in the shower. She was meeting Izzy downtown at the gallery where Kristen was having her art show. Izzy mentioned that Rick was going, too, which surprised Mia. It didn't seem like his kind of event. He'd mentioned once while she was staying there that he hated going to 'artsy-fartsy' events where people had to get all dressed up and everything was overpriced.

Izzy and Rick were just outside the gallery when Mia arrived and they walked in together. Andrew, the gallery owner, greeted them at the door. He was also the brother of Kristen's boyfriend, Tyler. Izzy's shop was just a few doors down from the gallery.

"Hi, Izzy. Good to see you again, Mia. And Rick?" Rick nodded, and Mia thought she caught a hint of a smile. "Kristen is in the back room, and there are glasses of Prosecco that were just poured. Help yourselves."

They made their way through the gallery and into the

big main room. Kristen was there with Tyler, and she was chatting with several people who were eager to meet the artist. Izzy handed Mia and Rick glasses of Prosecco and they slowly made their way around the room, looking at the various paintings. One wall was all Kristen's work.

They were gorgeous watercolors. This collection was mostly the ocean, cottages, flower gardens and rose bushes and brightly colored boats in the harbor. The colors were stunning and light seemed to glow from within the painting.

Mia saw one that she could picture over the cream-colored sofa in her living room. The blues and pinks of the flowers spilling over a white picket fence were so vivid and pretty. She stepped closer to check the price and was glad to see that it was in the range she'd anticipated. Expensive, but not outrageously so. She could afford to buy this one painting as an investment in her condo.

"Are you going to get that one?" Izzy asked.

Mia nodded. "I love it."

"It's beautiful. You may want to let Andrew know ASAP, though. I saw another couple eyeing it too."

"Good idea." Mia saw Andrew walking their way and quietly told him she wanted to buy the painting.

"Excellent. Did you want to take it home tonight or come by tomorrow?"

"I'll come by tomorrow morning." Mia handed him her credit card, and he returned a moment later with a slip for her to sign. "Here you go and thank you. It's a beautiful piece."

Rick raised his eyebrows when Mia walked back over

to them. "Did you actually buy one of these paintings? Such a waste of money."

"Rick!" Izzy glared at him.

"What? It's the truth. But, hey, it's her money, right?"

"Let's change the subject, please. How would you guys feel about walking over to Oath Pizza and getting a slice when we leave here?" Oath Pizza was a fast food gourmet pizza shop where they made slices to order.

"Can we go now?" Rick asked.

"No. We just got here. That would be rude."

"I agree that would be rude. The pizza does sound good, though." Will walked over in time to hear Rick's comments.

"Hey, Will." Mia was glad to see him.

"Hi, Mia, Izzy." He nodded hello to Rick, too. They chatted with Will while Rick sipped his Prosecco and looked bored. He perked up a little when Kristen came over to say hello.

"Mia just bought the blue flowers painting," Izzy told her.

"You did! That's one of my favorites. Thanks so much for coming." She chatted with them for a few more minutes until a new group of people came looking for her, and she had to resume her post and answer questions. Kate and Jack arrived a few minutes later and waved hello to Kristen, who was surrounded by potential customers.

"She has a good crowd tonight. Hopefully she'll sell lots of paintings," Kate said.

"Well, she's sold at least one." Mia smiled and glanced at her painting.

"You bought that one! Very nice."

A waitress carrying a tray of stuffed mushrooms got their attention as she walked towards them. They all took a mushroom and a few minutes later, she made the rounds again. Izzy was about to reach for a second mushroom when Rick shot her a withering look. "Are you sure that's a good idea?" he asked.

Izzy hesitated and took a step back. "Right. Probably not."

Mia glanced at the two of them in confusion. "Why isn't it a good idea? They're delicious. I'm having another one."

Izzy looked like she was wavering, but then Rick explained, "Izzy's gained some weight and said she wants to lose it. And if we're going for pizza after this, maybe she doesn't need a second mushroom."

Mia was speechless, and Will looked like he wanted to punch Rick. "It's a mushroom. If Izzy wants one, she should have one," Will said.

Izzy smiled gratefully at Will. "Thanks, Will. Rick is right, though. I really don't need another one. Not if I want to lose this weight. And I do."

"You look great, Izzy. You don't need to lose weight." Mia was furious with Rick. Her sister once had an eating disorder, and it had taken several years of therapy for her to have a normal relationship with food again. Rick seemed to know just what buttons to push.

"I've lost my appetite," Izzy said quietly. "Can we

walk around and look at more of the paintings? I might want to buy something, too."

Rick made a face. "We don't need any of these over-priced paintings in my house."

Mia was glad to see a bit of fire come into Izzy's eyes. "Your house? We both live there."

"Whose name is on the lease? Not yours," he snapped back. Will and Mia exchanged glances and Izzy looked mortified.

"Rick, please don't do this. Not in public. Let's have a nice night."

"You have a nice night. I'm going home. Your sister can give you a ride."

"Fine. I think that's a good idea. Maybe I'll see you later tonight, maybe I won't."

Rick looked confused and even more annoyed. "What does that mean?" He glanced at Will, who had taken a protective step closer to Izzy. "Where are you going?"

"If you're going to be in this kind of mood, I'm not sure I want to deal with you. I might stay at Mia's."

Rick sighed. "Just come home when you're ready, Izzy. I'll probably be in bed."

He left, and Mia breathed a sigh of relief. Rick was like a scowling ball of tension.

"I'm sorry about that," Izzy said to Will, who stared at her in amazement.

"Izzy, you have nothing to be sorry for. I know he's your boyfriend, but he seems like a real jerk. You can do better."

Mia nodded. "I think you know I agree with Will. I

haven't said much, as I know he's been going through a lot. But it doesn't seem like things are getting any better."

Izzy sighed. "They're not. I thought this new job might calm him down some. He's working with a good friend and it seems like things are going well, but he's always in a mood lately. Or he's really up, but the littlest thing can change it just like that. It's exhausting."

"I move back into my condo next week, if all goes well. You could move in and take my spare bedroom. There's plenty of room."

"I'm actually finishing up with your unit on Tuesday. I'll get your furniture back in on Wednesday and then you can move in as early as Thursday," Will said.

"Oh, that's good news. Thank you. Izzy, what do you think?"

"I'm almost there, but I'm not totally ready to give up yet. Don't hate me, but I do still love the guy. Though lately, I'm starting to wonder why."

"I could never hate you. You know the offer's always open. The spare bedroom has your name on it. Do you want to come home with me tonight and let him cool off?"

"I don't think so. He said he'll probably be in bed when I get home. Hopefully he'll wake up in a better mood. But, I'm going to have a heart-to-heart with him tomorrow and tell him things need to change."

CHAPTER 17

M ia went to breakfast a little before nine on Sunday. She was looking forward to seeing Lisa and hearing how her trip went. She had thought Lisa said they were going to be back for Kristen's show Friday night, but she didn't see her there and forgot to ask Kate if she was still coming. She saw both Kristen and Kate the next morning, though, as they had been filling in for Lisa while she was gone, making sure the breakfast room was stocked each day. They let her know that Lisa and Rhett decided to stay an extra night and were due back late Saturday afternoon.

When Mia stepped into the dining room, she saw Lisa right away. Rhett was just getting up to leave. Mia said a quick hello to him before bringing a plate of scrambled eggs, toast and her black coffee over to where Lisa was eating a grapefruit.

"Sit down and join me. Rhett had to go, but I'm not in any hurry."

"Good, I'm dying to hear all about your trip."

"Oh, it was wonderful. So relaxing. We went every-where, saw everything and ate so much. We went out for every meal. That's why I'm eating a grapefruit now."

"Did you see his other restaurants?" Mia knew that Rhett owned several restaurants that were well known and successful.

"Yes, we ate at all of them and I was impressed. He has a good team in place with each one. His daughter, Michelle, runs one of them, his first flagship restaurant. We saved that one for last, and she came with us. It was nice to spend some time with her where she lives. She gave us a tour of her city. Well, Rhett knows it well, of course, but it was all new to me."

"That sounds like a great trip. I'm glad you had a good time."

"Thanks, honey. We really did. We haven't taken any time off, either one of us, since we met. Not more than a day here or there, so it was nice to get away. Oh, and we toured some New York vineyards. You would have loved that. There are some good wines coming out of New York. We brought a case home, so you'll have to come some night when I have the girls over."

"I'd love that. Oh, Kristen's art show seemed to go well. I found a painting there for my living room. And it looks like I'll be able to move back in on Thursday."

"Oh, that's wonderful. Sooner than expected?"

"Yes, a little bit. Will had a cancellation, so he was able to get started sooner. I have to admit, though, I'm going to miss being here. I've really enjoyed having breakfast with you."

Lisa smiled. "I'm going to miss it, too. You'll have to stop in sometime for breakfast so we can catch up."

"I'd like that."

"So, what are you bringing to Kate's cookout later today?"

Mia laughed. "I'm so boring. I always bring the same thing, but I know it's good. My guacamole and chips."

"Well, I love guacamole and I haven't tried yours yet. I'm actually making a new recipe. It's something they serve at one of Rhett's restaurants—Honey Pepper Coconut Shrimp served with a creamy mango sauce."

"That sounds amazing."

"We'll see how it turns out. You'll all be my guinea pigs."

When Mia finished eating, she cleared her plate and said goodbye to Lisa.

"See you later today at Kate's. I'm looking forward to trying your guacamole."

Mia smiled as she headed up to her room to get her purse before going to the grocery store to pick up what she needed to make the guacamole. As she was going up the stairs, Ben was coming down and stopped when he saw her.

"I feel like I haven't seen you all week. I was starting to wonder if you'd already moved out, but then each morning, your car is here."

Mia laughed. "I was telling your sister that we seem to

have opposite schedules. She was asking if I'd seen you. She said you were racing in the Figawi."

"It was awesome. A buddy of mine has a boat, and I went to the Cape Friday night and sailed back Saturday morning with him and his crew. We head back first thing on Monday."

"That sounds so fun."

"Do you like to sail?"

"I've never done it before. The fast ferry is as close as I've come to sailing."

Ben was quiet for a moment, then grinned. "Do you have plans Monday?"

"Memorial Day? No, just relaxing. Why?"

"Why don't you sail back with us? We can have lunch at Baxter's, people watch for a while, then fly back. It will be a blast."

Mia hesitated for a moment. She was slightly nervous to go on a giant sailboat, knowing nothing about how to sail. But then she realized it was an opportunity she shouldn't pass up. "I'd love to. As long as you don't think I'll be in the way?"

He laughed. "Wait until you see the size of the boat and then remember that you said that. There's going to be a whole crew sailing it. You can sit back and enjoy the ride. The weather is supposed to be perfect. You can't say no."

"I'm not saying no. I'm in."

"Great. I'll knock on your door at a quarter to nine. Boats leave the harbor at nine-thirty sharp."

"I'll be ready."

MIA ARRIVED AT KATE AND JACK'S HOUSE A LITTLE AFTER three. There was already a good crowd gathered. The first person she saw to say hello to was Lisa's friend Paige, who lived just a few doors down. She was there with her boyfriend, Peter. Kate smiled and walked over when she saw Mia.

"Thanks for bringing the guacamole. You can put it on that table with the other munchies. Then help yourself to whatever you want to drink."

Mia handed her a bottle of chardonnay.

"Oh, thank you, I'll add it to the collection. If you want to open it, there's a wine opener by the box of ice."

Mia set her guacamole and bag of chips on the table next to a platter of coconut shrimp with a creamy orange dipping sauce. She guessed that was from Lisa. She opened the bag of chips and emptied them into a plastic bowl that she'd brought as well and then went to pour herself a glass of wine.

She saw that Izzy was already here, too, and was chatting with Will. There weren't any white wines open yet, so Mia opened the chardonnay she'd brought and poured herself a glass. She saw that Lisa was chatting with Kate and Kristen, and she walked over to say hello.

"We missed having you in Boston," Kate said to Lisa. "But I'm glad you had such a good time on your honeymoon."

"And I'm so glad you finally found a dress. I was getting a little worried," Lisa admitted. "But, I knew you were in good hands with Mia and Beth, and at least I'd had a chance to go with you here on Nantucket."

Kate laughed and turned to Mia. "We went everywhere here. Every possible place that might sell wedding dresses. We saw them all. I was hoping we'd get lucky and find something, but realistically I knew we'd probably end up going to Boston and I'm glad we did. The dress I found was perfect, and it was a really fun day."

"It was," Mia agreed. "And productive. I'm thrilled that both you and Beth found dresses that you're both excited about."

"Beth and Chase are coming, aren't they?" Lisa asked.

Mia glanced around and didn't see either of them.

Kate nodded. "They are. Beth called to say they're running a little late. They stopped down at the pier to say hello to one of Chase's friends that sailed over for Figawi weekend. Someone he went to college with, I think."

"Have any of you sailed in the Figawi?" Mia asked.

"Kate did, years ago," Lisa said.

Kate smiled. "I was a senior in college. I was dating someone whose CEO had a boat in the race and he got to invite someone to go. It was an experience. If you ever get the chance to go, you should do it."

Mia grinned. "I am, actually. My neighbor, Ben, invited me to sail back to Hyannis with them on Monday, then fly back later that afternoon."

Lisa looked pleased by this news. "Ben Billings? How fun. I had a good feeling about the two of you."

"Are you dating?" Kate sounded surprised.

"No, nothing like that. We're just neighbors and friends."

"That's the best way to start, as friends. Take some pictures, if you think of it. You can show me at breakfast on Tuesday," Lisa said.

"Oh, Sam's here. Mom, look how cute his girls are!" Kate walked over to greet Sam, who had his two girls with him, one on either side, holding his hands. Kate was right, they were very cute. They were wearing matching pink flowered sundresses and orange flip flops, and they both had their blonde hair in a ponytail with a pink ribbon tied around it.

Sam handed Kate a six-pack of Sam Adams IPA and a paper bag. "That has all the fixings needed for s'mores."

"Great, thanks. I love s'mores. I bet the girls do too, right?" The girls just stared at her.

"Becky, Sarah, this is my friend Kate. We grew up together, and this is her mom, Mrs. Hodges, and my friend Mia. Mia goes to the group with me on Wednesday nights. Say hello, girls."

"Hi," they both mumbled. But then Becky perked up and asked Kate, "Do you have hot dogs?"

Kate laughed. "Yes, of course. And burgers, too. Are you hungry?"

"I would like a hot dog, please."

"Well, I can help you with that. Follow me and we'll get you fixed up."

Kate led Sam and the girls over to the grill area, where Jack was taking burgers and dogs off the grill and moving them onto a big platter. There were bowls of potato and pasta salad, potato chips, coleslaw and various condiments. Everyone made their way over, made a plate and found somewhere to sit. Kate and Jack had set out extra chairs on the lawn, and there was a long picnic table and a big round table as well. Mia noticed that Izzy and Will were deep in conversation and hadn't gone for food yet. Sam and the girls were at the picnic table and Mia walked over to them.

"Do you mind if I join you?"

"Please, we'd love that. Wouldn't we girls?" They both nodded, but neither said anything.

"They're not usually this shy. I think it's a little over-whelming, maybe with all these people," Sam said.

"Or maybe we're just hungry, Dad." Becky smiled and then took a big bite of her hot dog.

Sam shook his head. "Becky's definitely not my quiet one."

"How's your burger, Sarah?" Mia asked. Sam's other daughter hadn't said a word, but seemed to be enjoying her food.

"It's really good!"

"We went and saw some big boats come in yesterday down at the pier. That was fun, wasn't it, girls?"

"It was awesome! We saw some of the biggest boats ever. It was so cool," Becky said.

Sarah nodded. "It was. We're going again tomorrow to see them take off."

"It was fun. I haven't seen the Figawi madness in years. I forgot how crazy and busy it is down at the pier."

Mia smiled. "That's one of the things I love about my condo. Izzy usually comes over at some point over the weekend, and we can watch it all from my deck."

"That must be fun. I bet you're anxious to move back there. Any word on when that might be?"

"This Thursday, actually. Will is finishing a little ahead of schedule, which is great."

"Can we go walk around?" Becky and Sarah were both done eating and bored with sitting.

"Take your plates to the trash can on the deck. Then yes, you can go exploring, but don't leave the yard."

Becky jumped up and Sarah followed. They ran to the trash can and dumped their plates, then took off roaming the big yard which led down to the ocean. From where he sat, Sam could keep a good eye on them. He'd barely touched his own food and turned his attention to it, polishing off a hot dog and a burger.

"They seem like great girls," Mia said. They were cute and well-behaved.

"They are. I'm lucky."

They chatted easily while they ate and Mia learned that Sam was a big reader, too. He liked mostly mysteries, and they liked some of the same authors. He was a big fan of Kate's, of course, and he'd read every book that Philippe had written.

"The Nantucket Book Festival is coming up in a few weeks. You should go. Izzy and I usually check it out. There are always local authors doing signings and a big gala one of the nights, if you like that kind of thing. Some vendors I work with usually have extra tickets, so sometimes we go."

"That sounds fun. Maybe we'll check it out. They do something under a big tent, too, don't they? Maybe the girls and I will find some kids' books. They love to read, too."

"I think they might."

"You know, I've been thinking about the conversation at the Rose and Crown the other night. Ken seems like he's ready to start getting out there, and it hasn't even been a year for him. I'm thinking that maybe it really is time for me to do the same thing. I still think of Mary all the time, and I'm struggling a little with feeling guilty for even thinking about wanting to get out more. The other part of me thinks it's overdue, and she'd want me to do it. What do you think?"

"I've been thinking a lot about it, too. And I understand feeling guilty. I wasn't with Mark as long as you were with Mary, but we were just two weeks away from getting married. It's been hard to let go of that and to even think about moving on. It feels disloyal, scary even. But I'm not as scared as I used to be by the idea of it. Maybe that means we're a little closer to taking that step?"

"We might be. I'm glad you're coming to the group. The group has really helped me a lot. And I look forward to going out afterward." He grinned. "That bereavement group is the closest thing I have to a social life these days."

"I've only gone a few times, but it has already helped me. Just listening to everyone and knowing we all have similar struggles. And that it really does get easier. It's a good group."

"So, I've been also thinking, maybe we should do something together? It might be good for both of us."

"It might be. What did you have in mind?"

"Well, I saw that Monday is trivia night at the Nantucket Culinary Center. I thought that might be kind of fun—something to do. Looks like they serve a simple dinner at six and then trivia starts at seven."

"That could be fun. I do like trivia." It had been over a year since she'd been, and she missed it.

"Good. So, we'll plan on a week from tomorrow, then?"

"Daddy, look what we found!" Becky and Sarah came running over, breathless and all excited about what Becky had cupped in her hands. She opened them slowly, and a tiny frog hopped out.

"Very cute!" Sam approved.

"Is it time to make the s'mores yet?" Sarah asked.

"I'm not sure. Why don't you girls go ask Kate. She's in charge."

"Ok, let's go," Becky said and raced off with Sarah close on her heels.

"They have so much energy," Mia said.

Sam laughed. "Don't I know it. They keep me on my toes."

Mia looked up and was surprised to see Rick walk across the lawn. She hadn't realized that he wasn't already there. She looked around and saw Izzy sitting with Will, Kristen, and Tyler. Rick made a beeline for them, and even from a distance, Mia could see that his expression was stormy. She immediately tensed, worrying about Izzy. Sam noticed it and asked, "What's wrong?"

"Nothing. It's just my sister. Her boyfriend just got here and doesn't look like he's in a great mood. They've been having some issues lately."

"I'm sorry to hear that."

Mia watched as Izzy stood and went to talk to Rick, heading off a possible scene. They spoke for a few moments and whatever she said calmed him down. She led him to where the food was. He made a plate and joined them.

"Oh, looks like the girls are waving me over. Time to make s'mores. You interested?"

"I'll be over in a few minutes. I want to go say hello to Izzy first."

"You want to make sure she's all right."

Mia smiled. "That, too."

SHE WATCHED SAM HEAD OFF TO MEET THE GIRLS AND went to visit with Izzy and the others. She'd really enjoyed talking to Sam and was looking forward to their night out Monday night. She knew neither one of them were ready to think of it as a date, but maybe it was a step in that direction.

She pulled up a chair and joined the conversation at Izzy's table. She was relieved to see that things seemed fine. Izzy was smiling and Rick was even talking and laughing with the others. Will looked like he was having a good time, too.

"How are you doing?" Mia asked Will when there was a free minute and the others were laughing about something.

"I'm good. I think honestly, our breakup was long overdue. I thought I was going to be more upset and not want to do anything for a while. But I'm actually feeling better than I have in a long time. Life is pretty good, I have to say. And I might even be ready to get back out there, which surprises the heck out of me."

"Really? That's great news. Do you have anybody in mind?"

Will was suddenly very quiet. "No, not really. But I'm optimistic that there's someone out there for me."

Mia smiled. "I have no doubt that there is."

"What about you? Is there anyone in your life yet?"

"Not really. Not yet. But I am starting to get out more, too. So, I think that's a good thing."

"Mia, do you want a s'more?" Becky was suddenly by her side, holding out a perfectly made, still warm s'more.

"Yes, I'd love one. Thanks so much, Becky."

"I made this one for you." She held it up proudly.

"You did a really great job on this. It's perfect." Mia picked it up gently, while Becky beamed and waited for Mia to take a bite. She bit into it and gave Becky the thumbs-up, and she ran back to where Sam and Sarah were toasting more marshmallows on the grill.

"That looks good. I think I need to go make one."

Will left and Mia turned her attention to Izzy, who was finally looking her way. Rick was talking with Tyler.

"Are you having fun? You looked deep in conversation with Will earlier. I didn't want to interrupt."

"I am having fun. Will and I hadn't really talked in a while. It was good to catch up. He seems like he's over Caroline pretty quickly."

"I think they were both over each other, but neither realized it until it was almost too late. He seems happier now than I've seen in a long time."

"He does, doesn't he?"

"Is everything okay with Rick? He seems like he's in a good mood, but I wondered when he got here so late," Mia asked softly.

"It's all good. He had to work late, and he didn't like seeing me sitting with Will. But I set him straight. We're all friends here, and he has no reason to worry about me. He calmed down fast. I think he was really just tired. He didn't expect the job they were on today to go so late. But it's a Sunday, so it was double-time and he couldn't pass that up."

"Right, it would be hard to say no to that."

"You looked cozy with Sam and his girls. Is anything developing there?" Izzy asked.

"I like Sam. We've become good friends. We have a lot in common, even beyond the bereavement group. We're going to go to trivia a week from Monday."

"Trivia. You and Mark used to love to do that." She paused before asking, "Is it a date?"

"I'm honestly not sure what it is. I don't think he's

sure, either. For now, it's just a fun night out. I have plans with Ben tomorrow."

That surprised Izzy. "You do? What are you doing?"

"You'll love this. He invited me to race back to Hyannis on his friend's sailboat."

"You're going on a Figawi boat? Wow. I'm impressed. That's a huge step out of your comfort zone. Is there any romantic interest there?"

Mia smiled. "No. Not at all. Ben's gorgeous and fun, but he's strictly a friend and a neighbor. He's just really fun to hang out with, and I think I need that right now."

Izzy nodded. "I think you do, too. I'm really glad that you're going out with both of them. Just out in general. I think it will be good for you."

"I do, too."

CHAPTER 18

Mia was ready when Ben knocked on her door
at a quarter to nine the next morning. She'd
gotten up early, went to breakfast at eight
and had a nice chat with Lisa and Rhett. Then she took
Penny for a walk on the beach, and showered and
changed. She wasn't sure what proper attire was for a sailboat race, so she dressed casually in jeans, a t-shirt with a
light blue sweatshirt from Izzy's store and her pink Sperry
topsider boat shoes.

"You ready to go? This is going to be fun." Ben was
dressed similarly in jeans, a navy sweatshirt and an ACK
baseball cap. ACK was the airport code for Nantucket
and was commonly seen on hats, t-shirts and sweatshirts
all over Nantucket.

Ben drove them into town and parked in his spot at
the condos, and they walked over from there. Parking was
at a premium in downtown Nantucket, so they were lucky
to have their parking spots.

There was a huge crowd gathered along the pier to watch the boats take off. The boat they were sailing on was moored out in the harbor and they were going to hop on a water taxi to get out to it. Ben led the way to where they would wait in line for the next available ride. It was almost their turn when Mia heard a familiar young voice call her name. "Mia! Dad, that's Mia!"

She turned and saw Becky and Sarah running toward her with Sam walking quickly behind them.

"Where are you going?" Becky asked.

"Are you going for a boat ride?" Sarah added.

Sam said nothing, but looked curious to hear Mia's answer.

"I am. We're taking a small boat to get to a bigger sailboat that belongs to my friend Ben's friend." She turned to Ben. "This is my friend Sam and his daughters, Sarah and Becky."

"You're going on one of these big boats?" Sam looked at Ben and then back at Mia.

"Which one are you going on?" Becky asked.

Mia realized that she had no idea. "I don't really know. Which one are we going on?" she asked Ben.

"That red one, straight out, next to the smaller blue boat."

Mia's jaw dropped. She knew some of these boats were big, but the one they were going on was massive.

"Wow. How big is that boat?" Becky asked.

"That's a fifty-footer," Ben said as they were directed to move up and get onto the next boat.

"Say goodbye, girls. We can wave as they sail off."

"We'll wave, too," Mia said as she followed Ben. They climbed onto the small boat that was shuttling people back and forth. A few more climbed in, the boat took off and a few minutes later pulled up beside the big red boat. Ben climbed off first, and then took Mia's hand and helped her onto the sailboat. His friend Nate and the rest of the sailing crew were already there. Ben introduced Mia, and showed her around the boat and where she should sit when they got underway.

Ben chatted with the others while Mia looked around and took it all in. The harbor was full of boats, all getting ready to go. At a few minutes before nine thirty, Ben told her to take her seat and tossed her a life jacket to put on. She zipped it up and settled into her seat, feeling a sense of excitement. A moment later, the whistle blew, and the race was on.

Mia saw the girls waving furiously and she stood and waved back as they began to move.

The boat glided out of the harbor and quickly picked up speed as the crew members expertly raised the spinnaker, turned the boat into the wind and the boat surged forward, cutting through the waves and sending a spray of water flying through the air, splashing across Mia's face. She laughed as it caught Ben, too.

"This is something else, huh?" he asked.

"It's amazing."

"Sit tight. I'm going to see if I can help."

Ben went to help the others as they steered the boat,

tacking back and forth into the wind, to keep their speed up.

At a certain point, Ben came back to let her know that the race part was over and now they were just continuing on to Hyannis, where Nate kept his boat at the Hyannis Marina.

"When we sail, it's not in a straight line," Ben explained. There's a lot of back and forth to catch the wind. So it takes longer."

Mia didn't care how long it took. She was happy, feeling the sun on her face and the wind in her hair and the occasional misting or heavy spray of water as they cut across the waves. It was loud on the water, with the wind whistling so she wasn't able to talk much to Ben, and he was busy helping the others as much as they'd let him. By the time they entered Hyannis harbor the wind had died down, and they pulled the spinnaker in and slowed way down. Mia always loved the view as she entered Hyannis harbor on the ferry, with all the gorgeous waterfront homes and the other boats coming and going. Even though it was the same view, it was even more exciting somehow from the sailboat.

Nate had a slip at the Hyannis marina and they smoothly glided in to his spot. Several of the crew members hopped out once they reached the dock and helped pull the boat into position and tie it up securely. Mia unzipped her jacket and handed it to Nate. "Did you have fun?" he asked.

"Yes. Thank you for letting me tag along. This was really amazing."

He grinned. "I never get sick of it."

Nate and one of the other guys both had cars at the marina. Ben and Mia rode with Nate and they all headed to Baxter's Boat House, a restaurant and bar that was just a short drive away and right on the harbor. It was busy there, but they were able to get two tables side by side that were right at the dock's edge. Mia had been to Baxter's once before and was happy to be there again. They were close to the water and some people even came by boat, pulling up and docking right in front of where they were sitting.

A waitress came to the table and everyone ordered Bloody Mary's, which Ben said was a Figawi weekend Monday tradition. Mia sipped her drink and watched the boats go by. There was a steady stream of them, all shapes and sizes, coming and going in both directions. It was a beautiful, sunny day, perfect for boating.

"Did you ever think about getting a boat?" Mia asked as another gorgeous boat cruised by.

"See that one?" Ben pointed to the boat she'd just been admiring. "That's a Sea Ray. I was here one day with Nate, years ago. We'd had a few drinks, and I saw one of those pass by and decided that I wanted one. Nate took me to the marina. They have a show room there and I came this close to buying one."

"What stopped you?"

"Nate did, actually. He knew it was just an impulse. He said the only people that should buy boats are people that are crazy about them, and that will take the time to learn how to fix them if something goes wrong.

And he said things always go wrong when you least expect it."

Nate leaned over and added, "I told him that he'd be smarter to just find a friend with a boat and then he wouldn't have to worry about any of that."

Ben winked. "So that's why we're still friends. I just got my boat fix for a while."

They ordered a bunch of food when the waitress returned. Baxter's mostly served seafood, and they were known for their fried clams.

"Any interest in sharing a fisherman's platter with me?" Ben asked.

"Sure." Mia didn't eat a lot of fried food, but at least once or twice every summer she indulged and a fisherman's platter had a bit of everything—fried scallops, shrimp, fish and clams, plus fries and onion rings. Their food came out quickly, and it was a fun time, eating outside, watching the boats go by and feeling the warm sun on her face. Mia had a second Bloody Mary and by the time they all finished eating, she was full and a little sleepy.

Nate dropped them off at the Hyannis airport, and they didn't have to wait long for their Cape Air flight back to Nantucket. Mia had mixed feelings about these small planes. They only held nine people, including the pilot. She was just glad that it was a short flight.

She gripped the arm of her seat as they taxied down the runway.

"Nervous flier?"

"I am. I flew in one of these small planes once when it

was raining. Izzy and I both watched as the pilot pulled out a laminated list of instructions and we both panicked, thinking he didn't know what to do next and it was some kind of cheat sheet. We learned later that it was just a routine checklist."

"I love to fly. My college roommate had his pilot's license, and we went up a bunch of times. He was a little crazy. We'd get up there and would be gliding around nice and smooth, and then he'd put it into a dive and start doing tricks, loops and rolls."

"Were you terrified?" Mia would have been.

"I probably should have been. But, no. It was exhilarating."

Mia looked outside as the plane picked up speed and then, like a bird, lifted up and they were on their way. She relaxed a little once they reached their cruising altitude.

"Thanks for inviting me along today." She knew she'd always remember the day. It was an experience she might never repeat.

"I'm glad you came. I like spending time with you, Mia. And I'm looking forward to being neighbors at the condos soon, too."

"When are you moving in?"

"Will said Friday should work for me. You're Thursday, right? Once we're settled, we'll have to celebrate. Maybe have a joint open house and invite all of our friends over."

"That might be fun!" Mia liked the idea. She and Ben chatted easily for the rest of the short flight. She glanced out the window and was surprised to already see

Nantucket coming up below. A few minutes later, they made a smooth landing. Ben called an Uber, and it wasn't long before they were back at the inn and climbing the stairs to their rooms. Mia thanked him again when they reached their floor.

"It was nothing. I'm glad you were able to come. Sleep well, Mia."

CHAPTER 19

The rest of the week was a busy one as Mia prepared to move back into her condo. The good news from Will was that he was able to salvage most of the furniture and paintings that he'd put in storage to work on. And she had the new painting from Kristen that she had in her room at the inn, all wrapped and waiting to be unpacked and hung once she moved back in. She was ready. She and Penny had enjoyed their weeks at the inn, but now that the move-in day was set for Thursday, she was eager to get home and sleep in her own bed.

When she arrived at the yoga studio for the weekly meeting, Ken was setting out his latest creation, lemon cake this time with lemon frosting. Mia brought a contribution this time, too. She'd stopped at the Italian bakery and picked up fifteen mini-cannoli. There was no sign of Sam by the time Janie called for everyone to take their seats. But at the last minute, he came rushing through the door, apologizing, and took a seat next to Mia.

They started the meeting, as usual, with everyone sharing how their week had gone. It was a long holiday weekend and for most of the group, that meant fun times with friends and family. For Candy, it was still a bit of a struggle.

"I did have fun this weekend, too, for the most part. I saw some friends I hadn't seen in a long time, and there were parties to go to every night. I kept busy, because I knew if I stayed in, that I'd just be sad. Last year, we had so much fun together, and it just isn't the same without him. And I felt a little guilty for not being sad enough, and for having fun. That probably sounds crazy."

The others assured her that it did not.

Then it was Mia's turn to share. "I had a good week. For the first time in a long time, I didn't have any sad days, even though it was a holiday weekend. I saw friends and family, and I stepped way out of my comfort zone and went with a new friend on a very big sailboat."

"That's a big step. Embracing new experiences and spending time with new people. Good for you, Mia," Janie said.

"I have some news to report." It was Ken's turn next. "I decided I was tired of eating alone and I invited one of the ladies that has been bringing me food to go out to dinner with me this weekend. I told her what was what, not to get any ideas, that I'm not looking to get married again, probably ever. And she still said yes. So, I'm taking her to the restaurant at the airport Saturday night. She likes to go there, too, and we can watch all those fancy planes take off." Many of the rich summer residents flew private jets and there was always steady traffic, especially on the weekends.

"That sounds like a good time, Ken. Sam, your turn."

"It was a mostly good week for me, too. The girls and I went to a cookout and had fun watching all the big boats down at the harbor. My mother offered to watch the girls pretty much whenever I want, so I'm going to take her up on that and try to get out more."

"I think that sounds like a good plan, Sam."

Later, when the usual group was at the Rose and Crown nibbling on the appetizers they'd ordered, Sam asked how her sailing day had gone.

"It was a great day. An incredible experience. Did the girls have fun watching all the boats leave?"

Sam smiled, but Mia had noticed he was a bit quieter than usual. "They did, and they were suitably impressed that they knew someone on one of the biggest boats there." He paused and then asked, "Who is that guy to you? The one that brought you on the boat? Are you dating?"

"Ben? No, we're not dating. He's my neighbor. And I'm planning his sister's wedding."

Sam relaxed a little. "Ah. Your neighbor at the inn?"

"Yes, and soon at the condos. He recently bought the unit next to mine. The only two that were damaged in the fire."

"Oh. Are we still on for next Monday night? For trivia?"

"Absolutely. I'm looking forward to it."

MIA'S FINAL BREAKFAST THURSDAY MORNING WAS bittersweet. She was excited to move back into her condo, but was going to miss chatting with Lisa and Rhett over her morning coffee.

"Once I'm settled, Ben and I talked about having an open house the same day and having all of our friends and families come by. I'd love to have you over."

"I think that's a wonderful idea, and I'd love to see your condo. It's such a beautiful spot."

"And I can't wait to hang the new painting I bought at Kristen's art show. I think it's going to look great in my living room with the white sofa and new hardwood floors."

"It sounds lovely. And you and Ben doing it together. That's very…neighborly of you. Are you sure there's nothing to explore there? He seems like a catch for the right girl."

Mia smiled. Lisa couldn't help trying to play matchmaker.

"I really like Ben, but it's not like that. He's fun and a good friend. He's definitely attractive, and if he were year-round on Nantucket, I might be tempted. But he's made it clear that he's not interested in being here much once the summer season ends. I think he'd be bored out of his mind in the winter. Ben is out every night. His real home is in the city."

Lisa nodded. "A lot of people feel that way. You're sure you couldn't see yourself ever moving back there? And just spending time here in the summer?"

Mia shook her head. "I'm not even remotely interested in that. I love the seasons here, the quiet of winter when there are no tourists, and it's just year-rounders. This is home to me."

"That's how I feel, too. I can't imagine living anywhere else."

LATER THAT EVENING, MIA POURED HERSELF A GLASS OF chardonnay and sat on the deck of her condo, with Penny curled up at her feet. She watched a gorgeous sunset over the water, watched the gentle waves rippling through the harbor, and she watched the boats coming and going. Will had done an amazing job. There wasn't even a hint of smoke smell, and the walls were all newly painted. Between that and gleaming hardwood floors, the condo almost looked brand new. And Kristen's painting looked perfect hanging just above her cream sofa. It added a splash of vivid color to the serene feeling of the room, with its white walls and windows that looked out over the harbor. Mia sighed with happiness. It was good to be home.

CHAPTER 20

Ben moved in the next day and was in and out, meeting with various movers and delivery people. Mia's move had been much simpler as everything she owned was in Will's storage facility, and he had insisted on overseeing the move since everything had been with him. So, when she'd walked in, it was almost like she'd never left, except everything looked shiny and new.

Ben, meanwhile, was coordinating with movers that brought some things he had in storage, his bed, and TV. He also had bought furniture for the rest of the condo—sofas, a dining table, another bed and bedroom furniture for the spare room. Mia was going to invite him over for a drink once he was finished, but he stopped by instead for a quick hello on his way out to meet friends.

"Are you around tomorrow?" he asked. "I told Bethany I'd give her girlfriend Alexis a few pointers. We have a tee-time at four at the club. We could use a fourth and I suggested you, if you're interested. She thought it was a great idea. You can just share her clubs again. We're only going to play nine-holes. Bethany had no interest in playing eighteen."

"Sure. I could do that." Mia liked the idea of playing with other people who were beginners.

"Great, see you tomorrow then."

THE NEXT DAY WAS A BEAUTIFUL DAY FOR GOLF. IT WAS perfect Nantucket weather, sunny and around seventy-two degrees with a slight breeze. Mia had gone shopping earlier in the day and bought her first golf outfit—a bright pink golf shirt and a white golf skort that looked like a skirt over comfortable shorts. She even splurged and bought a pair of golf shoes and a Lilly Pulitzer visor that was a tangle of pinks, purples, and blues over a white background.

Ben nodded in approval when he saw her.

"You look great. This is going to be fun."

They were meeting Bethany and Alexis at the club and when Mia stepped inside, she was immediately reminded of the club her parents belonged to in the Hamptons. There was an aura of obscene wealth and people that were used to it. Bethany and her friend Alexis arrived a few minutes later, and it was immediately apparent to Mia that this was meant to be somewhat of a setup for Alexis to spend time with Ben.

Alexis was a beautiful girl. Mia guessed she was late

twenties, a few years younger than Bethany. She had long blonde hair and an enviable figure, full in all the right places but with a tiny waist and a flat stomach. Mia stood up a little taller and was glad her new skort had an elastic waist. Mia wasn't overweight, but she'd never be as thin as Bethany and Alexis and she didn't mind too much. She didn't want to worry about every bite she put in her mouth, the way she knew Bethany did. She enjoyed food too much for that.

"So, are we ready?" Ben asked.

He led them out to where the golf carts were. "Mia and I should probably ride together, since we're sharing clubs, right?" Bethany asked with a sweet smile.

Ben hesitated for a second before saying, "Sure, of course. Alexis, you can hop in with me."

After Ben and Alexis drove off, Bethany followed them and as they rode along she said, "Alexis recently broke up with her boyfriend. She needs to meet someone new. I thought she and Ben might get along. She lives and works right in Manhattan, too."

"Oh? What does she do?"

Bethany laughed. "As little as possible. Her father is a mucky-muck at some investment company and she works for him."

"And she's never golfed before either?" Mia was starting to feel nervous as groups of golfers walked by.

"Never. And I've only been out a few times. I'm pretty bad."

"Won't we hold everyone else up?"

"We would, if we played the way they do, but Ben will

have us play best ball. Whoever hits the best shot, we'll move our balls there and that will keep things moving along."

"Oh, good."

They followed Ben's cart to the first tee, and Ben gave them all a quick lesson on how to swing. He went first, and they all watched in awe as his club made a loud cracking sound as it hit the ball and then it soared, going so far and fast until it finally landed way down the fairway. Bethany went next and wasn't as bad as she had led Mia to believe. Her ball didn't go as far as Ben's but it was nice and straight.

Alexis stepped up, swung and missed. Mia was glad to see she wasn't the only one that happened to. She hit on her third try, though it didn't go very far and landed in the rough just off the fairway. Finally, it was Mia's turn, and she took a deep breath as she stepped up to the tee. She tried to keep in mind everything that Ben had taught her—arms straight, eyes on the ball, keep her feet down. She swung hard and connected well with the ball, and it landed just behind Bethany's.

"Good job, you guys. Now pick up your balls and bring them down to mine and we'll hit from there."

It took them just under two hours to play nine holes and when Ben suggested an after-game drink in the club house, they all happily agreed. Ben ordered a round of drinks for the four of them and they took their drinks to an outside table. Bethany chatted about her wedding, with Alexis asking questions now and then. But she seemed more interested in Ben than in the details of Bethany's wedding.

"Are you heading back to the city after the wedding?" she asked him.

"No. I'm not anxious to get back there yet. The fall is still gorgeous here. I was thinking probably just after Columbus Day weekend, so mid-October."

Mia hadn't realized he planned to stay that long.

"You don't have to get back sooner for your work?" she asked.

He grinned. "There's some flexibility about that when you work for yourself. I can do a lot online."

"I bet you'll get bored after Labor Day when most of the tourists leave," Bethany said. She turned to Mia. "Don't you get homesick in the winter? This place is like a ghost town."

Mia shook her head. "I'm used to it now. I get back to the city now and then to visit my parents. That's enough for me."

"Mia and I were talking about having a co-open house soon. Now that we're both back in our condos. How does next Saturday work, Mia?"

Mia had nothing planned. "That works for me."

"Good." He looked at Alexis and Bethany. "You'll both come?"

Alexis pouted. "I won't be here then. I'm heading home on Friday."

"I'll be there."

"You guys live next to each other?" Alexis looked as

though she was wondering if there was something more going on. "That must be nice."

Ben smiled. "It is. I got lucky having Mia as a neighbor."

THEY FINISHED THEIR DRINKS, SAID GOODBYE TO BETHANY and Alexis, and drove home.

"Do you have any plans for dinner? I thought maybe we could grab a pizza and eat on the deck. Have another drink and celebrate being home."

"Sure. I'll call it in. What do you like on your pizza?"

"I'll eat just about anything. Pepperoni is always good."

Mia called an order in for a large pepperoni pizza from the place around the corner from their condos. By the time they got back there, it was just coming out of the oven. Mia insisted on buying the pizza since Ben had treated to the drinks and the golf game.

Mia handed the pizza to Ben and went home for a minute to change into a pair of jeans and took Penny outside so she could do her business. She put a plate of food down for Penny and walked next door to Ben's condo. His door was ajar, so she knocked and pushed it open. She had a bottle of chardonnay with her and saw that Ben was getting out some paper plates and napkins.

"Wine glasses are in the cupboard by the sink."

"Do you want me to pour you a glass?"

"No, thanks. I'm going to grab a beer." He took a

bottle of Sam Adams out of the refrigerator, and they went out onto his deck with their drinks and the pizza. His unit was a mirror image of hers, but his decorating was much darker, more masculine. He had brown leather sofas and a huge, flat-screen television that took up most of the wall.

She followed him onto his deck and sat in one of two padded chairs at a table just big enough for the pizza box and their plates. Ben put a slice of pizza on two plates and handed one to her.

It was a gorgeous night. The slight breeze from earlier had stilled, and the harbor was as smooth as glass, with the boats reflected on the surface. They bobbed gently in the water, and the sound of the waves lapping against the shore was music to Mia's ears. It was her favorite sound.

"I never get sick of the sound of the waves."

"I don't either. Though the first night I slept here, I had the window open and had to close it after a while. It was almost too loud."

Mia smiled and took a sip of her wine. "It was like that for me at first, too. You'll get used to it fast."

"So, you're sure Saturday night works for you, to have some people over? I was thinking around six or so, keep it casual. I can pick up some Bubba burgers and hot dogs."

"That works. I can make some pasta salad, and of course guacamole and chips. And I'll pick up some wine and mixers."

"I'll get beer and vodka and maybe more cups and paper plates."

"I'm sure people will bring stuff too. Kristen usually

brings either brownies or her peanut butter chocolate chip cookies, and Kate and her mom love to cook and always make good appetizers."

They were quiet for a moment, and then Ben asked, "What made you decide to move here? To leave the city for good?"

It was a more serious question, and Mia took a moment to think about how best to answer.

"It was impulsive and yet it wasn't. Izzy and I shared a house here one summer when she'd just graduated and I was on break. I was an elementary school teacher then, and it was my second year teaching. Having summers off was the best part of that job."

"You didn't like teaching? I could see you doing that. You have a calming way about you—especially with my sister. I know she's not the easiest at times."

"I didn't love teaching. Not like I thought that I would. I loved being with the kids, but dealing with the parents and the school system itself was frustrating. I kind of fell into the wedding planning. A friend that worked as an assistant for one of the biggest companies in Manhattan got married and moved to Colorado and recommended me for her job. She thought I'd be good at it, that I might like it, and I did."

"Okay, so that must have been busy and exciting in the city. How did you end up here?"

"I followed Izzy. She'd gotten a job right out of school in the management training program at Macy's. It was a great opportunity, and she learned a lot. But Izzy was always more of a free spirit, not the corporate type. We took another vacation together that summer, only for a week because neither of us could get much time off. We stayed right downtown at the White Elephant and had a blast playing tourist all week.

We did a lot of shopping and one day we walked into the store where Izzy is now and they were hiring. An older woman owned it and she and Izzy hit it off. She hired Izzy on the spot. Izzy gave her notice and found a room to rent and off she went. We were both living at home then. And once she left, I didn't want to be there without her. But I realized I didn't want to rent a place in the city, either.

My mother thought I was nuts, but I gave my notice, too, and told my boss that I was moving to Nantucket and would appreciate any referrals she wanted to send my way. I was half-joking, as I figured I'd get a job waitressing somewhere to pay my bills while I tried to get a wedding planning business off the ground. But two weeks after I moved here, I got a phone call with a referral. A small exclusive wedding and they wanted me to handle it."

"So you never had to get that waitress job? Nice."

Mia laughed. "Oh, no. I did. I worked at the Straight Wharf for a year until I had enough steady bookings that I could go full time with wedding planning. It's hard to explain, but both Izzy and I fell in love with Nantucket. Have you ever gone somewhere and instantly felt like you could live there?"

"Yeah. That's how I felt when I visited San Francisco for the first time. There's just something in the air there. It's hard to explain. It's always comfortably cool and often misty and breezy and yeah, I could imagine living there. If I wasn't in Manhattan."

"So, you know what I mean then."

"Yeah, I guess I do." Ben lifted his beer and held it out towards hers. "Well, cheers to both of us finally being home."

CHAPTER 21

Sam came by to pick Mia up for trivia Monday night at a quarter to six. She gave him a quick tour of her renovated condo and he marveled that there had ever been a fire.

"It looks brand new. You must love it here."

"Thank you. I do."

They arrived at the Nantucket Culinary Center a few minutes before six. Mia had heard of it but hadn't been before. There was a cafe, and they also did community open mic nights and art talks in addition to the weekly trivia. They gave their name at the hostess stand and were led to a table. The trivia nights didn't have a full menu, just whatever dish was on for the night and the cost was only five dollars plus whatever else you drank. Tonight, the dinner was vegetarian chili with cornbread. Mia ordered a glass of Bread and Butter chardonnay and Sam had a draft beer.

Mia noticed that Sam looked a little nicer than usual. Something was different.

"Did you cut your hair?"

He grinned. "Yes. It was long overdue. Does it look all right? I went to my dad's barber."

"It looks good." She'd thought he looked good before. She couldn't place his cologne, but she liked the smell of that, too, and she didn't remember him wearing any before. He wore a navy button-down shirt and what looked like new jeans. She'd made a little extra effort, too. She'd tried on several outfits before deciding on her oldest, softest jeans and a thin cotton sweater in a pretty shade of turquoise.

"You look really nice, too. I like that color on you."

"Thank you." The waitress brought their drinks right over and then just a few minutes later, their bowls of chili and cornbread arrived.

"Do you miss living where you were before this?" Mia knew he'd lived in a suburb outside of Boston, but didn't remember which town it was.

"Do I miss Waltham? No. Not at all. It's fine if you work in the city, but I'm much happier here. The girls are, too. What about you? Ever have second thoughts about moving back to Manhattan? How did you end up here, anyway?"

"No second thoughts. Ever." Mia told him the story she'd told Ben, and Sam looked intrigued.

"You used to be an elementary teacher? I don't know why I'm surprised. You were good with the girls. They really liked you. Becky was very impressed with the big red boat you went on."

Mia laughed. "They're great girls. You did a good job with them."

"Thanks. It wasn't all me, though. Mary was a stay-at-home mother, and I used to travel a lot more. That's something else I've started to think about with regard to getting back out there and dating. It's not just me. I'm a package deal with the girls. That rules me out for a lot of women."

"I don't know about that. You might be surprised."

"You really think so? This is all new to me. You wouldn't mind dating someone that already has kids?"

"To be completely honest, I've never thought of it before now. But, no. If I liked someone, I'd understand that it was, as you put it, 'a package deal.' But, I might want to have one or two kids at some point, too, so whoever I date would have to be okay with wanting more kids."

"That's understandable. I have a feeling the girls might love being older sisters and babysitters, eventually. I haven't really thought about it either, but I'd be fine with more kids."

As they finished eating, the trivia host came around to welcome them, and to take their team name and hand out pencils, a scoring sheet and a small notepad for their answers.

"What should our team name be?" Sam asked.

Mia thought for a minute. "What about Janie's Yoga?"

"I like it. It's more upbeat than bereavement and it gives Janie a little promo."

They spent the next two hours playing team trivia, answering questions from different categories. There were twenty teams playing, and from the laughing and teasing that they saw between some teams, it was clear some of them were regulars. Mia had never played trivia here before, but for quite a while she'd been a regular at the Rose and Crown for trivia night. Thinking about it brought a sudden wave of sadness that took her by surprise. The sad moments had been fewer and farther between lately.

"What's wrong?" Sam noticed that she'd grown suddenly quiet.

"It's just a little bittersweet, being here, and playing trivia. I haven't played in over a year. Since Mark died. It was one of our things. We used to go almost every week to the Rose and Crown."

"I'm so sorry. We could have done something else."

"Oh no. I'm glad we came. It was just such a big part of our lives that it just made me sad for a minute. It also made me realize how much I missed it. It's a fun night out and something to do mid-week."

"I can't think of anything else I'd rather do on a Monday night," Sam agreed.

They made a good team, and by the end of the night were pleasantly surprised to find themselves in third place before the final question. But Mia knew that the final question often knocked out people who were in first place. It all depends on what the category was and how sure you were of your answer. And sometimes, even when you think you knew it, it turned out you were way off. They blew the final question and ended up with a score in the middle of the pack.

"Seinfeld questions always trip me up," Mia admitted. "I feel like they should be easy and I've seen all the episodes."

"I know. But there were so many seasons. I do the same thing. It's easy to mix things up. It was still fun, though. I'm glad we came. Are you?"

"Yes, I'm glad you suggested it."

It was just about nine when Sam pulled up in front of Mia's condo. "So, same time next week? Are you up for a repeat?"

Mia grinned. "Absolutely." It had been a fun night overall, and she'd enjoyed Sam's company. He was easy to be with and smart. He knew most of the geography and history questions that she always had a hard time with, and she did well with the science and entertainment questions. She was looking forward to playing again next week.

CHAPTER 22

The co-open house was a success. It was a beautiful, warm night and just about everyone they knew stopped by at some point that Saturday evening. Mia, of course, made her guacamole and pasta salad earlier that day, while Ben manned the grill, cooking up burgers and dogs for everyone. Lots of people brought additional food. Kristen made her famous peanut butter chocolate chip cookies, Lisa brought creamy homemade potato salad, and Kate had Jack pick up cooked shrimp and cocktail sauce on his way home from the seafood market.

Lisa had never seen inside the condos before and was suitably impressed.

"Mia, this is really lovely. And Will did a fantastic job. It looks brand new in here."

"I know! He really did." Mia smiled as Will walked over and said hello.

"Your ears must be ringing. We were just talking about what a gorgeous job you did."

Will blushed a little. "Thank you. I'm glad I was able to help. It was a fun project."

"Hey, Will. Lisa," Izzy said as she and Rick walked over. Will moved on after a moment to get a drink, while Izzy and Rick stayed to chat for a bit.

"The place looks really good, Mia." Rick sounded impressed and Mia was glad to see that he also seemed to be in a good mood. He laughed and chatted with Lisa, too, and Izzy seemed more relaxed than Mia had seen her in a while. She hoped that things were getting better with them.

Sam arrived soon after and handed Mia a bottle of Bread and Butter chardonnay. He also had a six-pack of the local Nantucket beer, Whale's Tale Pale Ale. Mia was touched that he remembered the kind of chardonnay that she liked.

"Thank you." She handed him one of the beers and put the rest in the refrigerator.

"I can only stay about an hour or so. My parents have dinner plans with another couple tonight. But I wanted to stop by. Your place looks great."

"Thank you. And I'm glad you were able to come, even if it's just for a little while. Come out on the deck. That's where the best view is."

Mia led him out onto her deck, where Kate and Jack were chatting with Kristen and Lisa. Sam said hello to everyone and admired the view.

"You weren't kidding. You must love being out here."

Mia smiled. "It's my favorite spot. I'm on the deck all the time, watching the boats as I drink my morning coffee or my evening chardonnay."

They both turned at the sound of the door opening from the unit next to Mia, and Ben stepped out with more burgers for the grill. He waved to everyone on Mia's deck and Sam frowned.

"He practically lives with you."

Mia laughed. "We don't actually see each other as often as you'd think. Ben is a good friend, but we have very different schedules. He's not much of a morning person and I go to bed early. He's a good neighbor, though. And we thought it would be fun to throw a party together."

"I suppose it makes sense. Since you both just moved back in and you know some of the same people. And he's just here for the summer, right?"

"Yes, Nantucket in the winter is not lively enough for Ben. He'll probably head back to the city not long after Labor Day is my guess."

Sam's hour flew by way too quickly and he had to get back home to relieve his parents.

"I really wish I could stay. But, we're on for trivia again on Monday?"

Mia smiled. "Yes, I'm looking forward to it."

She walked Sam to the door and rejoined the party, which went on for several more hours. Izzy and Rick were the last guests to leave, around eleven, and Mia was glad they'd stayed as long as they did. Rick was on his best behavior and she hadn't seen her sister this relaxed and happy in ages.

As soon as she finished cleaning, which didn't take too long, she took Penny out for a quick walk and waved goodnight to Ben. He was on his deck and people were still streaming into his condo. He tried to get her to join them, but she laughed.

"I'm off to bed. I'll see you later."

And when she climbed into bed, she cracked her window a little and could faintly hear laughter and music coming from Ben's condo. It sounded like they were having a good time, and she suspected his party might go until the wee hours. She yawned and snuggled into her pillow. She was just not a late-night person. It had been a fun evening, but she was very happy to be comfy in bed.

CHAPTER 23

A few weeks later, Angela surprised Mia the day before the Nantucket Book Festival Gala by calling to offer her two tickets.

"Philippe and I are flying out to LA this weekend and we won't be using the tickets. I thought you might want to go?"

"I'd love to. Thank you!" She hung up and immediately called Izzy to see if she wanted to go with her.

"Ordinarily, I'd say yes. But, I already told Rick I'd go with him tomorrow night to a party at his friend's house. He wouldn't be happy with me if I bailed on that."

"Okay. How are things going with him?" Izzy had been quiet on the subject for a few weeks, and Mia wasn't sure if that was a good or bad thing.

Izzy sighed. "It depends on the day. It's still up and down with him. But his job is going well and there have been more good than bad days lately. So, I'm optimistic and don't want to break that streak by going to the Gala. Although, I would love to go. Why don't you ask Ben or Sam? I bet one of them would want to go. It seems up Ben's alley. I think I've seen him there in the past."

"That's a good idea. I'll do that."

Mia ended the call and thought for a minute. Ben would probably say yes in a minute, if he wasn't already going. She agreed that it did seem like an event he'd enjoy. But she found herself calling Sam instead. She hoped that it wasn't too short notice for him to find a sitter.

"Hey, Mia, what's up?" He sounded happy and surprised to hear from her in the middle of the day.

"I don't know if this is too short notice for you to find someone to watch the girls, but Angela just gave me two tickets to the Book Festival Gala. It's tomorrow night. Any interest in going with me?"

"Oh, wow. Yes. I'd love to. Let me just check with my mother to make sure she can watch the girls and I'll get right back to you."

Less than ten minute later, he called back. "She's a little too happy to watch the girls. I told her I was invited to go to a black-tie event, and she was thrilled. She's funny."

Mia was glad that his mother seemed to approve of Sam spending time with her. They saw each other twice a week now, every Monday for trivia and Wednesday for the bereavement group meeting. Mia looked forward to both nights each week.

THE NEXT DAY, GETTING READY FOR THE GALA, SHE FELT nervous for the first time. Butterflies nervous, like when she went on her first early dates with Mark. She wasn't sure how she felt about that or what it meant. She tried to ignore the nerves and focus instead on what she was going to wear. She had a few dresses that would be appropriate —cocktail dresses she'd worn to various events in the past —but her eyes kept going to a black dress in the very back of her closet. A dress that still had tags on it and that she'd been unable to throw out or to wear. She'd loved the dress when she'd first seen it. It was a basic little black dress, sleeveless with a ruffled bottom that flared out at the knee. It was very flattering. But she'd bought it to wear to her rehearsal dinner.

She took the dress off its hanger and tried it on, then twirled in front of her bedroom window. It still fit, and it still looked good. And she didn't feel like taking it off. Instead, she found a pair of scissors, cut the tags off and found the new shoes she'd bought the day she found the dress. They were still in the box they came in, packed with tissue paper. She tried the shoes on, too. They were a delicate, strappy silver sandal with a medium-high heel. Just enough to give her a lift, but she'd still be able to walk without too much trouble. She kept the shoes on and went to do her makeup and fix her hair. She ran a curling iron through it to give it some soft waves, added a final swipe of pink lipstick and she was ready.

Sam arrived fifteen minutes later and at first glance, he took her breath away. She'd only seen him dressed casually before. He looked elegant and so handsome in his black suit and blue-gray silk tie. His shoes gleamed and his hair was lightly gelled and his eyes—had she never really noticed his eyes before? How green they were? Maybe it was the black suit, but it really made his eyes stand out. Especially when he smiled.

"You look beautiful, Mia."

The butterflies came rushing back. "Thank you. You look very distinguished and handsome, too. Let me grab the tickets and we can go." She found them in the kitchen drawer, put them in her small black evening bag and they headed out. They probably could have walked as the event was being held at the White Elephant, but it was a hot and sticky night and Mia didn't want to go too far in new shoes. Sam drove and when they arrived, handed his car off to the valet parkers.

There was a steady stream of well-dressed people making their way into the event. Mia looked around to see if anyone was there that she knew and smiled when she saw Ben and Bethany in line at the cocktail bar. She should have known that they'd be at this event.

They made their way in and went to get a drink. Ben looked pleasantly surprised to see them.

"Mia! I didn't know you'd be here. We have room at our table, join us after you get a drink. I'm buying, what can I get you both?"

"Chardonnay for me, thanks."

"I'll have a Dewar's and water."

Once they all had their drinks, Ben led the way to their table. It was a round table that sat ten people, and Bethany's fiancé and Alexis were there as well. Mia noticed with interest that Ben handed Alexis a drink and then sat next to her. Maybe Bethany's matchmaking efforts were paying off.

A few minutes later, though, Ben wandered off to talk to some friends and Bethany did the same.

"Do you want to walk around and check out the silent auction?" Mia suggested.

"Sure, let's go." Most of the silent auction items were signed first editions from authors that were participating in the book festival. There were a couple of lunches with the author, too. Mia noticed that Kate, Tyler and Philippe all had signed books up for auction and Philippe also had a 'lunch with the author'. He would host ten people at his Nantucket home, serve them lunch and answer all their questions. Mia smiled. She could picture him doing it. She looked around to see if Kate and Jack were there. She'd talked to Kristen the day before, and she'd said that Tyler wasn't up for going. He hated those kinds of events and Kristen wasn't a big fan of them, either, so they were staying home. But she said she'd thought Kate would be there. Mia had left Kate a message, too, but they hadn't connected.

The room was filling up fast. There was a good crowd and Mia was a little surprised at all the familiar faces she saw—authors that she recognized from the back of their book covers like Jodi Picoult, Nancy Thayer and Elin Hilderbrand.

"There you are! Kristen told me you were coming, and Sam, too. I'm so glad you guys are here." Mia turned around to see Kate behind her, looking gorgeous as usual in a sleek gold dress. Kate was so tall and slim that everything looked good on her. Jack looked sharp in his suit, but a little less comfortable than Kate was. Mia suspected that, like Kristen and Tyler, he'd rather be home but agreed to go because Kate wanted to.

"Did you just get here? I think there's room at our table. We're sitting with Ben and his sister Bethany."

"We just walked in. Lead the way. I want to put my stuff down and then get a drink."

The next few hours flew by and it was a really fun night. There was an elegant dinner, followed by music and dancing and the silent auction. They all needed to dance off all the food they'd eaten and as soon as the band started playing and the music was good, they made their way out to the dance floor. Mia and Sam danced and danced, one song after another, until they were exhausted and about to take a break, but then the music slowed and instead, Sam took her hand and pulled her toward him. And they swayed to the music. They were so close that she could smell his cologne and the butterflies came back again as he moved a hand to the small of her back to guide her around the floor. She was surprised by how his touch made her feel. It was like all of her senses were heightened. She snuck a peek at his face to see if his expression would reveal that he was similarly affected. His eyes met hers, the vivid green that was even more disconcerting up close. She looked away and took a deep breath.

"Are you having fun?" he asked softly.

"So much fun. Are you?"

"I am. More than expected. I'm a little hot, though. Do you want to take a walk outside and get some air after this song?"

"That sounds like a good idea."

When the music ended, Sam took her hand and led her off the dance floor and through a set of French doors that led outside. There was a nice breeze, and they leaned against the side of the building. Mia noticed that Sam was still holding her hand. She looked up at him and he smiled, and she found herself lost in his eyes again. Mesmerized by what she saw there.

They say the eyes are the windows to the soul and what she saw and felt was breathtaking. She understood, for the first time, that what Sam felt for her went beyond friendship. And she felt the same way toward him. It was like everything suddenly shifted and a world of possibilities opened up. She smiled back, an invitation extended. He accepted, leaned forward and touched his lips ever so gently to hers. Neither of them wanted the kiss to end, but finally they pulled apart.

"I didn't realize how long I've wanted to do that," he admitted.

"And I didn't realize that I wanted you to until now. I'm so glad you were able to come tonight."

"Me, too. I think we both owe Angela a big thank you."

Mia laughed. "We do. You can thank her at her wedding, if you like?"

"Are you inviting me to her wedding?"

"Yes. I'm technically working it, but she told me I'm very welcome to bring a date."

"So, that means we're dating now?" He had a twinkle in his eye.

"I guess it does."

"Ken would be proud."

Mia smiled. Ken gave them weekly reports on how his evenings out were going. He wasn't ready to call them dates yet. But he'd been out with the same lady, Ruth, several times now and talked about her all the time.

They went back inside and danced some more. When Sam took a break, Mia, Kate and Bethany stayed on the dance floor and when the music slowed, Ben got up and asked her to dance.

"If you don't mind," he said to Sam. "I want to borrow her for a minute."

Sam laughed. "As long as you give her back."

Ben led her around the dance floor and while he was an excellent dancer, Mia didn't feel the same way in his arms as she had in Sam's.

"Something's changed with you two. I don't have a shot anymore, do I? You like this guy?"

Mia nodded. "Yeah, I really do."

"Okay. Well if you get bored with him, remember you can always come back to Manhattan. We'd have a blast there."

Mia laughed. He was too much. "I'll keep that in mind."

Mia danced the last song of the night with Sam, and then he took her home and kissed her again at her door.

"I had a really great night. See you again on Monday for trivia?"

"I had a wonderful night and yes, I'll see you then."

CHAPTER 24

Mia had just changed into her pajamas and was getting ready to head to bed when her phone rang and it was Izzy. Mia's heart sank. If Izzy was calling her this late, after midnight, something was very wrong.

"Mia, are you home yet?" Izzy sounded upset.

"Yes, I just got in a few minutes ago. Where are you? What's wrong?"

"I'm on my way over. I hope that's okay. Will is driving me and we're just a few minutes away. I can explain when I get there."

"Of course it's okay. And you can stay as long as you like. I'll get your room ready for you." Mia hung up and went to check the spare bedroom. There were clean sheets on the bed. It hadn't been used since Mia moved back in. She turned the light on and folded the covers back, and the room was ready for Izzy. Mia got two towels and a washcloth out of the linen closet and laid them on the dresser for Izzy to use in the morning.

She heard footsteps coming up the stairs and went to open the door. A clearly shaken Izzy and a concerned Will walked in.

"Can I get you something to drink? Hot tea, water?" Mia offered.

"A hot tea would be nice," Izzy said.

"Anything for you, Will?"

He shook his head. "No, I'm all set."

"You guys have a seat. This will just take a second and then I want to know everything." Will and Izzy went into the living room and sat on the sofa while Mia made a cup of tea for Izzy. It only took a minute or so and she brought it to Izzy, who accepted it gratefully.

"So, what happened? Start from the beginning."

"Well, I mentioned to you the other day that things were going well for a change, and I wanted to keep that going so I went to the party? Rick's still been moodier than ever, and I thought going to this party with him might help. And it was fun at first. I didn't know many people there, so when Will walked in, I was glad to have someone to talk to. Rick was off in the other room talking with his work buddies and I'd been trying to get to know some of their girlfriends. But they weren't overly friendly."

"I'm friends with the guy that had the party. He's sent some jobs my way recently," Will added.

"So anyway, as the night went on, everyone was drinking and Rick was having margaritas instead of his usual beer. One of the guys made a big batch, and they were all drinking them. I tried a sip, but they were too strong for me. Will and I were hanging out chatting and Rick came into the room and lost it." She lifted her sleeve and showed Mia deep red marks on her right arm. Mia gasped. "Rick did that to you? Tonight?"

"He did. He's never touched me before, but he grabbed me by the arm, hard, and dragged me outside and screamed at me. Accused me of all kinds of nasty things, but the gist of it is that he was jealous that I was talking to Will and insisted that I was cheating on him— with Will. I told him he was out of his mind."

"I went outside after them because I was worried for Izzy's safety. He's twice her size, and he was pissed off," Will said.

"He saw Will come outside, and he got mad again and grabbed my other arm and tried to drag me to the car to take me home." She pulled up her other sleeve and there was a matching set of ugly red marks from where Rick had squeezed her arm hard.

"I went after them then and gave Rick a taste of his own medicine," Will said.

"What did you do?"

"I hauled off and clocked him hard right on the jaw. He let go of Izzy, fell over and we ran off."

"Wow. Izzy, you can't go back there. Ever."

"I know that now. It took me a while to get here, but he crossed a line with me. And you were right. Rick's anger issues aren't getting any better, and I don't feel safe around him anymore."

She sighed and put her head down so that Mia couldn't see the tears that suddenly overwhelmed her. Mia jumped up and rushed over to her sister. She pulled her into her arms and gave her a gentle hug, being careful not to touch where she was sore and bruised. "Go ahead and cry it out, Izzy. You have nothing to be ashamed of. This is all on him."

"She's right, Izzy. You're much too good for that guy." Will stood. "I should probably get going. Izzy, if you need anything you let me know."

Izzy nodded and looked up through teary eyes. "Thank you, Will. I don't know what I would have done without you. You're a good friend."

A strange look passed across Will's face before he smiled and wished them both a good night.

Once he was gone, Mia made herself a cup of tea, too. She'd been exhausted earlier, and now she was wide awake and worried for her sister. She didn't think they'd seen the last of Rick.

CHAPTER 25

The rest of the summer seemed to pass in the blink of an eye. Before Mia knew it, August had arrived and she had two weeks of back-to-back weddings. Bethany was up first on the fifteenth and a week later, it was time for Angela and Philippe's wedding. Izzy was still living in Mia's spare bedroom and planned to stay at least until the end of the year before looking for her own place. Mia wasn't in any hurry to see her go. She liked Izzy's company and felt she was safer for now, living with Mia.

Rick, as predicted, didn't take Izzy's leaving well. He alternated between ranting and raving and sending flowers and apologizing. But this time, Izzy wasn't having any of it. She was devastated, but remained strong, and Mia was proud of her for it. Finally, after more than a month, Rick finally seemed to accept that Izzy wasn't coming back, and he stopped calling.

Things were going well with Sam. They both agreed

that it was best to take things really slow and to hold off on telling the girls that they were dating. Sam wanted to wait until some time had passed and they were really sure about the direction that things were going before he told them, and Mia understood that. Neither one of them was in a rush. They were enjoying their Monday and Wednesday nights out, and now they added in either a Friday or Saturday night on most weekends. Mia knew that Sam's mother was rooting for them and that she was thrilled that Sam had found someone.

Bethany's wedding went off without a hitch, although there was one glitch when the goats almost didn't make it in time for yoga. The woman who booked goat yoga had an event in Chatham and they were due to come back on Saturday, but the boats stopped running because of high winds. Fortunately, the seas were calm in the morning and they made it onto the first ferry over and there was goat yoga after all at Bethany's brunch. Mia smiled, picturing all those tiny goats running around on the Fast Ferry. She got some funny pictures for Bethany at the brunch of the goats hanging out on people's backs while they held various yoga poses. She thought it was the strangest thing, but it was all the rage evidently.

Ben brought Alexis to Bethany's wedding, and it seemed like the two of them really were hitting it off. Alexis flew over most weekends and usually stayed with Ben. And now he was talking about heading back to Manhattan after Labor Day weekend instead of staying until October.

Angela's wedding was a size and scale that Mia had

never seen before. No expense was spared. They decided to offer a unique wedding favor that also in a way made things easier for everyone, too. The six hundred and fifty blue and white folding director style chairs that were carried down to the beach were the wedding favors. They told each guest to take one home when they left. There were a few stray ones left behind, but overall the chairs were a huge hit.

And Angela was a beautiful bride. She looked elegant and effortlessly beachy in her white JCrew slip dress. Philippe looked great in his purple tux, and it seemed like all of Nantucket was there. Mandy did a fantastic job overseeing the catering and the food, as usual, was delicious. They got married on the beach, with all their friends and family around them and Philippe had buses shuttling people to and from his house, because there wasn't nearly enough parking anywhere for a wedding that big.

Sam came as Mia's date, though she wasn't able to spend much time with him until the ceremony and meal service was over and the dancing began. A few hours later, platters of mini burgers and fries were brought out, and they were a huge hit. People were hungry again after dancing and drinking.

It was a wonderful night and Lisa and Rhett were among the last to leave the dance floor.

"This was spectacular. You and Mandy did an incredible job," Lisa said. Mandy and Mia were relaxing with a glass of wine. Mandy still had the catering clean-up to oversee, but she had time to take a short break.

"Angela and Philippe look so happy," Mia said. Angela was glowing and Philippe couldn't stop smiling.

"Won't be long before it's Beth and Chase's turn and then Kate's. It's going to be a busy fall," Lisa said.

As the party started to wind down, Mia ran into Izzy and she looked exhausted.

"I'm going to head home, I think. I'm beat."

"Are you feeling okay?" Mia asked.

"I'm fine, just tired. I'll see you a little later."

By the time Mia left, it was almost midnight.

When she walked in the door, she expected Izzy to be in bed, but she was sitting on the living room sofa, with her legs crossed, Indian-style, and her eyes were red. She looked up when Mia walked in and smiled. And then she started to cry.

"What's wrong?" Mia put her purse down and went to her sister. She looked like a mess, like she'd been crying for some time before Mia got home.

Izzy reached next to her and held up a pregnancy test stick. "Can you believe it?"

"You're pregnant?" No wonder Izzy had been looking so tired lately.

"I've had the test for a few days. I put off taking it because I wasn't ready for the news. But after the wedding, I couldn't wait any longer. I've felt bone tired this past week, like all I want to do is crawl into bed and I've wanted to eat everything in sight, except watermelon. I can't stand the thought of watermelon now, isn't that strange? And my bras are suddenly too tight. That's never happened before. I think I knew what the result was going to be before I took the test. I just had to prepare myself for it."

"Oh, Izzy. How are you feeling about this? Besides not feeling well."

"I dread having to tell Rick, of course. But I'm not upset about being pregnant. I'm actually excited to have this baby. I love it already. My emotions are just all over the place."

"I'm going to be an aunt. And Izzy, you have to stay here now. Don't even think of looking for a place until after the baby comes."

Izzy smiled. "I hoped you'd say that."

CHAPTER 26

To no one's surprise, Rick didn't take the news of his impending fatherhood all that well. He went through various stages beginning with rage, and more accusations that the baby wasn't his to his most recent stage which was the most concerning to Mia. He was now in love with the idea of being a father and was determined that Izzy should come back to him, for the sake of the baby, so they could be a family. So far, Izzy was staying strong, but now and then, Mia knew she was wavering and considering the idea of going back to Rick. Rick claimed he was a changed man and that he was going to start going to anger management classes. To his credit, he did sign up for them and started going. It was a twelve-week program, so to appease him, Izzy said she'd reassess when he finished.

And that twelve weeks would be up just before Kate's wedding, the first weekend in December, same time as the Nantucket Stroll. Mia reminded Izzy more than once that she didn't have to give him an answer the minute he finished the course. It would be wiser to wait a few more weeks and see how he did after that.

In the meantime, Izzy wasn't even showing yet, so she hadn't told anyone the news. She wanted to wait until it was obvious and when ultrasounds had given her the all clear that everything was going well.

And Mia was excited to be going to a wedding that she wasn't involved in coordinating. Sam was on his way over to pick her up and they were heading to Beth and Chase's wedding. The service at the church was lovely, and Beth looked so beautiful in her lacy wedding dress. The church was walking distance to Mimi's Place where they were having the reception, so they all walked over. It was Columbus Day weekend and as it often was in mid-October, it felt like Indian summer with unusually warm and lovely weather.

Mia said hello to Mandy and Emma when they arrived, and then she and Sam took their seats. They were seated with Angela and Philippe, and Izzy and Will. Will and Chase often passed projects to each other, and Izzy and Beth had become friendly through Kate's get-togethers. Izzy and Will weren't dating, they were just friends, but Beth figured it made sense to put them all at the same table. And Mia sensed if it was up to Will, that they would be dating.

He didn't know about the baby yet. Izzy hadn't told anyone, but somehow Mia didn't think that would deter him. Will was around often, checking in on Izzy. The two of them had started coming to trivia on Monday nights, and they all had a good time together. Mia was hopeful that once Izzy was more settled that maybe something might develop with Will, possibly. But she knew her sister wasn't thinking along those lines yet. She was busy learning everything she could about how to be a good mother.

Mia had a feeling that both Sam and Will suspected what might be going on with Izzy, though. Izzy used to always have wine when they went out and now she only ordered soda water with lemon and while her stomach was still flat, her bras were overflowing and even though she tried to dress in a way that would de-emphasize that area, she was still looking curvier than usual. And guys tended to notice that, even if they didn't think about the reason why.

The food, of course, was excellent. There was eggplant and chicken parmesan and meatballs and beef braciola. There wasn't a band, but there was a really fun DJ with a great personality and excellent music choices. Soon after dinner, everyone was up on the dance floor. Lisa danced with Chase and was beaming, so proud of her son and his lovely wife.

Mia danced with Sam and loved swaying in his arms as they slowly moved around the dance floor to Eric Clapton's *Wonderful Tonight*. They had grown closer in the past few months and she was hopeful that maybe by Christmas, Sam might have a conversation with the girls and they might include them more when they went out. She didn't mention anything to Sam yet, but if he brought up wanting to tell the girls, she was going to suggest that they might take a trip to Boston for a night, to go see the Nutcracker and have dinner in the North End.

At the end of the night, Beth tossed her bouquet and everyone cheered when Kristen caught it. No one looked more surprised than she did, and no one more pleased than Lisa as Kristen would be the last of her four children to get married.

CHAPTER 27

"I think it's time you introduced Mia to the girls, don't you?" Sam's mother said one day while the girls were at dance class and Sam was visiting.

"The girls already know Mia," Sam teased. He knew what his mother was suggesting, and he'd been thinking that it was about that time, too.

"You know what I mean, Sam."

"I do. And I agree. I was planning to tell them soon."

"Good. Christmas is coming and I want to invite Mia and her sister to join us, since they don't have any family nearby."

"I'll mention it to her, but I don't know what their plans are, if they're going home to New York to see their parents."

"Well, as long as you extend the invitation, so they know they're welcome."

"I'll do that. Thanks, Mom."

SAM LEFT SOON AFTER TO GO PICK UP THE GIRLS. HE thought about Mia the whole way. Things had been going so well, almost too well. It scared him a little, but it also made him excited for the future. He pulled up in front of the dance studio and waited. A few minutes later, the girls came running out and raced over to the car. They both climbed in the back seat and buckled up.

"How was dance?"

"Good. What's for dinner, Daddy? Are we going to Grammy's?" Becky asked.

They always went to his mother's for dinner after dance class. It was a Tuesday night ritual.

"Yes, we are. She made spaghetti and meatballs, your favorite."

"Yay!"

"So, girls, I have something to tell you. You know my friend, Mia?"

"Wedding planner, Mia?" Sarah asked.

"Yes. That's the only Mia I know."

"What about her?" Becky said.

"Well, you girls like her, right?"

"Yeah, she's nice," Sarah said.

"I like her," Becky added.

"Well, I like her a lot, too. So, I've decided that she's going to be my girlfriend. How do you girls feel about that?"

"Will you kiss her?" Becky asked.

Sam did not anticipate that question. "I might. How would you feel about that?"

"It's okay with me, Daddy. Do you know if Grammy is making garlic bread, too? I'm really hungry." Sarah said.

"I'm hungry, too," Becky added.

Sam smiled. He'd been so worried about breaking the news about Mia, and the girls were more interested in what was for dinner. But at least they said they liked her.

"So, I told the girls about us," Sam said while they were sitting at the Rose and Crown after the Wednesday night meeting.

"You did? Were they okay with it?" Mia was eager to hear.

"They both said they like you, Becky asked if I was going to kiss you."

"What did you tell her?"

"I told her I might."

Mia smiled. "And what did Sarah ask?"

"She said it's fine with her, but did I know if her grandmother was going to make garlic bread for dinner."

Mia laughed. "Priorities."

"Right. Oh, and my mother said to be sure to tell you and Izzy that you're both invited for Christmas dinner. I told her I'd ask, but wasn't sure if you were going home to see your family."

"Oh, that's nice of her. We usually do go home

around Christmas, but this year my parents said they are actually going to be traveling so we're going to go see them the weekend before New Year's Eve instead, so tell your mother we'll happily accept her invitation."

"I'll do that."

"Oh, and since you mentioned Christmas, what would you think about taking the girls into Boston for a night to see The Nutcracker? We could stay the night and come home the next day."

"I bet they'd love that."

"Excuse me," Ken said.

Mia and Sam both glanced his way. They'd been caught up in their conversation, completely oblivious to the three others at the table. Janie, Candy and Ken were wide-eyed as they hadn't told them that they were dating, either.

Sam grinned. "Looks like the cat's out of the bag. Yes, it's official. We didn't want to say anything to you all too soon, since we're both still coming to the group meetings and weren't sure if there was some kind of policy against it."

Janie smiled. "I think it's wonderful. I'm happy for you both."

Candy and Ken both nodded in agreement.

"How are things going with Ruth, Ken?" Mia asked.

"Good. We're going to the Christmas Stroll together. I think we might start dating soon." He grinned, and they knew he was kidding. Ken and Ruth had been going out to dinner at least once a week for months now.

"I think we're all doing pretty good," Sam said.

CHAPTER 28

"I talked to Rick today," Izzy began. She was sitting on the edge of Mia's bed while Mia tried to decide what to wear for Kate's wedding.

"Oh? How did that go."

"Rick really wants to try again. He seemed so sweet and sincere, and he said the anger management classes have made him a new man. I don't know what to do, I'm really torn. And my hormones are all over the place."

"I think you should tell Rick that you'll make a decision once the baby comes. That will give you plenty of time to see if his best behavior sticks. And once you have the baby and feel back to normal, you can make a rational decision about what you want to do."

"You're right. I know you're right. He can just be so persuasive sometimes. But I'll tell him that. So, what are you going to wear?"

Since she was working this wedding as well as

attending as a guest, Mia had to get there early. The reception was at the White Elephant Hotel, which one of the prettiest wedding sites on the island. It could accommodate up to 275 guests and had gorgeous harbor views. Kate's wedding wasn't quite that big, but it was just over two hundred, which was still a good size. All of her mother's friends and Jack's father's friends were going, and both Kate and Jack knew a lot of people in town, too.

Kate was a foodie and went with a wide variety of options including raw bar, passed hot hors d'oeuvres, a pasta station and a carving station. Mia went over early to make sure everything was ready. And it was. She checked all the table settings one last time before walking to the church where Sam saved her a seat.

Just about everyone's eyes grew damp when the wedding music started and Kate walked down the aisle, escorted by Rhett. She looked stunning in the gown that fit her like a dream. Going to all those stores had paid off when she found the perfect dress for her. Jack stood waiting, and looked handsome and nervous right up until the moment they finished exchanging their vows and rings and the minister said, "And now you may kiss the bride!"

The hotel was just a few streets over and everyone walked except for Kate and Jack. Rhett had his antique car waiting for them out front with a 'Just Married' banner on the back window, and he and Lisa drove the wedding couple over to the White Elephant.

It was just starting to snow as they walked outside and it was also the Saturday of Nantucket's Christmas Stroll.

The streets were full of shoppers and the streets and windows of the stores were decorated for Christmas with twinkling lights and festive garlands.

Mia kept busy making sure things went smoothly at the reception, but there was less to worry about at a well-managed hotel like this and she was able to join Sam when everyone sat down for dinner. The food was excellent and there was an open bar so everyone, other than Izzy, was indulging and feeling very merry.

Kate made the rounds visiting with everyone and gave Mia a big hug when she sat down for a bit with them.

"I couldn't have done this without you. You know how stressed out I was. You made things so much easier. Thank you."

"It was my pleasure." And it was. Mia loved her job, and it was even more fun when it was a friend's wedding.

"I can't believe I was so nervous. Now that the day is here and we're married, I'm just really happy."

"Where are you going on your honeymoon?" Sam asked.

"We're going to the Cayman Islands. Jack loves to dive and snorkel, and neither one of us have been there."

"That sounds wonderful right about now." Mia looked out the window where the snow was starting to come down more heavily. "When is your flight?"

"It's not until Monday. We're going to spend the night in Boston tomorrow and fly out Monday morning. Weather forecast is clear for tomorrow, so we should be good."

Kate had a lively band and once the music started,

everyone was up and dancing. Toward the end of the night, Mia and Sam were slow dancing and enjoying the evening immensely and when the music ended and they were about to walk back to their seats, Sam said, "I never would have imagined last Christmas how much better things would get for me this year."

"I know. Last Christmas was pretty bleak for me. I didn't think I'd ever date again. Couldn't fathom it. I feel very lucky that Kate suggested I go to that bereavement group and that I met you."

"I didn't think I could love again. I really didn't think it was possible. But I was wrong." Mia felt a shiver as his words sunk in. He loved her!

"I was wrong, too. I didn't think it was possible either until I met you."

"Mia, look up!" Mia heard Lisa's voice and looked up just in time to catch the bouquet that Kate threw.

"Well, isn't that something," Sam said.

"If that isn't a sign, I don't know what is," Lisa whispered delightedly.

Mia had to agree. Finally, everything in her world felt full of hope and wonder, and she looked forward to what her future held.

THANK YOU SO MUCH FOR READING. I HOPE YOU ENJOYED Mia's story. Stay tuned for more in this series. Next up is Izzy's story.

Until then, have you read The Restaurant?

Coming soon is a historical saga, Gilded Girl and a sequel to The Restaurant, Christmas at the Restaurant.

And please visit my shiny new website and sign up for my newsletter.